# The Nile Delta
# Mystery

# The Nile Delta Mystery

MICHAEL BAUM

RESOURCE *Publications* · Eugene, Oregon

THE NILE DELTA MYSTERY

Resource Publications
An Imprint of Wipf and Stock Publishers
199 W. 8th Ave., Suite 3
Eugene, OR 97401

www.wipfandstock.com

PAPERBACK ISBN: 978-1-6667-4500-9
HARDCOVER ISBN: 978-1-6667-4501-6
EBOOK ISBN: 978-1-6667-4502-3

MAY 12, 2022 4:59 PM

We were slaves to Pharaoh in Egypt and Hashem our God,
Brought us out from there with a strong hand and an outstretched hand.

**THE HAGGADAH**

# CHAPTER 1

# THE TSUNAMI

A T 11.05 on October the 7<sup>th</sup> 2019, at latitude 32.2 and longitude 29.6, 7 km north of Alexandria, tectonic plates were shifting. The plates had been largely jammed against each other for centuries, and pressure built up. Finally, something gave. Hundreds of square miles of seafloor suddenly lurched horizontally some 160 feet and thrust upward by up to 33 feet. Scientists later called this a megathrust. Like a hand waved vigorously underwater in a bathtub, the lurch propagated to the sea surface and translated into waves. As they approached shallow coastal waters, their energy concentrated, and they grew in height.

This event happened to occur early in the winter season of the archaeological exploration of the sunken cities of Thonis-Heracleion and Canopis beneath the waters of Abukir Bay, at the edge of Egypt's north-western Nile Delta. In antiquity the western most branch of the Nile, the Canopic, flowed 30 kilometres east of Alexandria.

Less than 10 meters deep, Abukir Bay is easily accessible using conventional SCUBA (self-contained underwater breathing apparatus) equipment. During each excavation season the research vessel, Princess Duda, anchored over the area to be investigated. The vessel provided not only a home for the archaeological dive teams, but also space for the researchers to study the artefacts brought up out of the silt below. The excavations were conducted by small teams of divers working in shifts, which generally lasted around two hours. The dive time was limited both by the amount of air in the divers' cylinders and the physically demanding nature of their work. To reach the temples, monumental stones and statuary, the first task of the divers was to remove the overlying blanket of sand using a water dredge resembling a giant underwater vacuum cleaner. In 2001 to the east of Canopus about 6.5 kilometres from the coast the team discovered a harbour town on the West Bank of the former mouth of the Canopic branch of the Nile. Effectively, the whole site consisted of several islands with channels crossing it connecting the eastern harbours with a large western Lake. The widest transverse waterways were called by the research team, the North canal and Grand canal, gave access to wide openings in the lines of sand dunes that provided a sheltered anchorage at the ancient South East port and from there to the mouth of the main western tributary running into the delta and from there to the mighty Nile itself. It was easy to get lost underwater in this labyrinth during a sandstorm triggered by hoovering up the sands of ancient times. To avoid this hazard, every pair of divers would "buddy up" together with buoys on lines from their air tanks going up to the surface so that those on watch aboard Princess Duda, might keep an eye out for them. It was at the precise location and at this precise time, that David Goddard found himself. David was a very senior member of the crew, a very experienced SCUBA diver and a doctorate in studies of the Ptolemaic period of ancient Egypt, from University College London. In truth though he shouldn't have been there in the first place. His colleagues who respected his skills and expertise, all agreed that he was "Long past his sell by date". Although aged 55, he was reasonably fit but often drunk. He had lost his wife to breast cancer 12 months ago and had taken to drink by way of coping with his loss. Often his judgement had been impaired, and he could be reckless in extending his time underwater until his air tank was close to empty and then shooting up the shot line at the last minute ignoring the risk of the decompression sickness. Although at these depths the risk wasn't that great. The other divers were to cut him some slack at first out of sympathy, but when it came to risk the life of his buddy, it was time to let him go. This was in fact his last dive.

He first became aware of the tsunami rushing towards him, when the waters above his head divided, and he found himself standing on the wall of the old South East port having lost all buoyancy as the water level dropped below his knees. It took him only a fleeting moment to understand what was happening, then he smiled to himself behind his mask thinking, "What a way to go!".

The face of the tsunami wave hit him like a train engine and he lost consciousness, his last thoughts were "see you soon darling", yet when he was awoke he was not yet dead but rotating slowly in the central stratum of the fierce flow of the river water returning home from the depths of the earth. His senses told him that he was rolled into ball with his air tank and other equipment intact on his back, whilst the waters rotated around his vertical axis. At each turn he marvelled as the flood water shovelled up the sand in front of him, disclosing briefly the rock bottom of the Nile. After a while he was quite enjoying the ride, better than anything experienced at a theme park. This transient euphoria wore off quickly as he realised, he was running out of air, so once again he steeled himself to "kick the bucket". As the needle on the gauge of his SCUBA kit reached zero, the flow of the river slowed down and just before rising to the surface he did indeed see a bucket on the rock bottom. This bucket was made of gold and surrounded by other artefacts, the most impressive of which were the remains of a chariot. He thought he must be a hallucination as the mist of hypoxia took hold and silently his body heralded by his red and black buoy, rose to the surface, much to the alarm of a group of young Egyptians boys trying to spear fish from the East bank of the Nile.

Two of the boys pulled him to safety whilst the other two ran to fetch the elders from the nearby village, leaving the other buoy bobbing in the reeds, marking his point of ascent.

David slowly came to again and noted that for the second time he had avoided death on the Nile. His head ached, he was bruised all over and desperately in need of a double whiskey to calm his nerves. Although a scholar and an artist, he was in many ways a Bohemian. At the best of times he looked a mess, and this was not the best of times. He dressed like a tramp and seldom cut his long, prematurely grey, hair. As someone knowledge-able about art history, beyond the limits of ancient Egyptian iconology, he recognised that he had an uncanny resemblance to Rembrandt van Rijn. The bulbous nose, the ruddy complexion, the unruly hair and the apparel of the great master after he first lost his beloved wife Saskia; then his muse, housekeeper and model, Hendrickje Stoffels, his son Titus and finally his fortune. A late self-portrait of the old man, on view at Kenwood House in northwest London, is the spitting image of David Goddard PhD.

He tried to stand up without success as his legs turned to jelly and on looking around had no idea where he was. He tried to talk to the two boys standing guard over him, but they had no language in common. Slowly, wincing as each strap rubbed against a bruise, he removed his SCUBA gear from off his back and undid the belt holding emergency equipment. He then stripped off his wet suit causing him agony pulling the tight legging of his left ankle, only then did he realise that he had lost his flippers in the maelstrom. This left him near naked except for his thermal underwear and a waterproof belt around his waist. He then started shivering in spite of the hot sun. Propping himself up on the air tanks, he smiled at the boys and showed his compass, first aid kit and torch. To win their confidence and as a token of thanks he offered the boys his torch as a gift using hand signs, much to their delight. In return they offered him their hoodies that couldn't even pull over his head. He then dug around his emergency kit to look for his miniature flask that carried two drams of 16-year-old Lagavulin for emergencies only. To his dismay he discovered that he'd forgotten to top it up after yesterday's emergency. As it was every day had an emergency that justified emptying the flask. After about half an hour, the other two boys remerged from a mud brink wall 10 feet from the bank of the river, accompanied by two brown wizened old men from their village carrying blankets. Fortunately, one of the men spoke French having served in some mysterious way, with the French Foreign Legion. When he learnt that the name of the village was Naucratis, he knew precisely how far he travelled down the Canopic branch of the Nile Delta. He could barely believe that the tidal wave had carried him along for 30Km.

Naucratis was the name of an important city that reached its apogee in the 6th C BCE and remained the principal trading centre into the Ptolemaic period. At its peak, archaeologists deduced that there were about 10,000 citizens with many temples, palaces and well-built homes for the wealthy. The whole area had been explored by Flinders Petrie in the last two decades of the 19thC. Imports from the Mediterranean, from Greece and further away, were dropped off at the customs sheds in the harbours of Canopus and transferred to riverboats that sailed down the most western tributary of the Nile delta and offloaded at Naucratis, the most important trading centre in the north of Egypt. Today the outline of this city remains, whilst the current residents of the village bearing its name live in modest two-room buildings built of mud bricks plus the occasional granite or marble block stolen from the archaeological site. They don't have much of a tourist trade but earn their living sailing feluccas on the river transporting fish caught nearby or fresh food from the smallholdings along the riverbank.

The two old men from the village invited David to join them on their way back to their homes. As he stood up his left ankle gave away and he found it too painful to walk on his own.

He looked a pitiful sight, more like a drowned nude rat than a sub-aqua archaeologist, supported under his shoulders by two wizened old men followed by four boys carrying his gear.

On arriving at the village, the procession attracted the attention of the whole population numbering about 70 who poured out of their hovels. He was carefully settled on a charpoy under the shade of a date palm outside the home of one his rescuers whose name he learnt was Ali Ben something. Ali Ben then rushed into his house and brought one of his old gallabiyah to preserve David's dignity that wasn't improved very much, as it looked like a mini dress on his 6-foot frame.

A little old lady came bustling out of the mud-brick house carrying a circular brass tabletop that was balanced on a stand at his right side. Immediately behind her, was a younger woman wearing the black robes of mourning, who carried a tray with an elaborate swan-necked jug of sweet Arabic coffee and a plate of sweetmeats. The women urged him to eat and drink by flapping their hands. The coffee was very welcome and energised him enough to start contemplating the calamitous situation he found himself. He was in the middle of nowhere, he assumed that the support ship and its crew would have been lost in the tsunami, along with all his worldly possessions apart from the underwear he wore and had probably broken his ankle along the way. By way of mitigation, he remembered that he still had his waterproof money belt that carried $500 and his passport. He always carried this with him as there were native members of the crew recruited locally that he couldn't trust. Meanwhile, a huddle of the men was arguing amongst themselves in Arabic until a young fit, handsome youth, with brilliant white teeth, stood up and started talking to him in a passable mixture of pidgin and schoolboy English.

"'Allo' Mr Man from the Nile. You are most welcome in my village. You no look welly well and leg no good. Me am Ahmed and the old man here my grandfather. He big shot here and Mrs Grandmother wants you to stay but is worried about bad leg. We have truck will take you to General Hospital Abouhms in Abu Hummus." At this point he indicated north. With a big smile and applause from those standing around, he squatted down in front of David.

With great ceremony, David was carried to the clapped-out Fiat truck and lifted into the flatbed at the rear to make himself comfortable with the sacks of dates that were in any case ready to be transported nearby Abu Hummus. Ahmed jumped into the driving seat and his grandfather joined him upfront. With a crunch of the tiered old gearbox and his foot down on the throttle, they zoomed up north. Although the journey was only 10 Km the road along the east side of the river for most of the way, was a bumpy dirt track. Each bump rattled the bones in his left ankle, and he found it hard to suppress his screams.

They hit the paved road two kilometres south of Abu Hummus and David was pleasantly surprised to see a proper little modern town with proper shops and a newly built General Hospital, instead of some third world shantytown. He may have been very knowledgeable about ancient Egypt, but apart from the fleshpots of Cairo and Alexandria, he knew very little about the development of modern Egypt and that was why he was surprised to see the little town of Abu Hummus had so many modern amenities. His two guardians helped him hop along into the emergency department, which was mercifully quiet at this time. Later they learned that it had been very busy that morning as a knock-on effect of the tsunami 20 kilometres to the North. At the registration desk, Ahmed completed the formalities with a young woman wearing a hijab who was yet able to flutter her eyelashes at the bashful young man. After a short wait he was beckoned into a cubicle where a young Egyptian surgeon welcomed him a big smile and introduced himself as doctor Kareem Yacoub. David was lifted onto a couch and propped up to talk to the doctor. "I see from the registration documents that you are a doctor Sir, is that a doctor of medicine or a PhD?" David smiled "Yes you guessed, right, I have a doctorate in Egyptology". "Well that's really interesting, where did you study this subject?" asked Dr Yacoub. "At the most famous Department of Egyptology in the UK, University College London, and if I might ask, where did you learn such perfect English?". "At my medical school in Alexandria, where all the subjects are taught in English and in addition I studied for a postgraduate doctorate at, the National centre for Orthopaedics in Stanmore north London, an affiliate of University College London!".

"Well what a remarkable coincidence. We've both been awarded doctorates at the same university and furthermore I know a lot about the medical school in Alexandria in the period 400–300 BCE". They both enjoyed a laugh whilst Ahmed and Ali Ben looked on in amazement not understanding the reason for this mirth.

At this point Dr Yacoub shooed them out the room and carefully and gently examined David's left ankle, that was now obviously bruised and very swollen. He had a light touch but when he came to try to move the ankle the pain for exquisite. He stopped at that and said, "I must now send you for an X-ray as I suspect you have a fracture of the ankle or at least torn ligaments." "By the way, I nearly forgot to ask you how you came to twist your ankle so badly?" The young doctor looked on with incredulity etched on his face as Dr Goddard told his tale. Once his finished telling his story Dr, Yacoub responded, "You must be the luckiest man alive or you have been blessed by the God of the Nile, Hapi and happy thou shalt be." The visit to the radiology department was uneventful and by the time he returned to the clinic, Dr Yacoub was already examining the digital image on this desk top computer.

He then beckoned to the porter who had wheeled the patient to and from the X-ray room, to bring him over to inspect the images. "Well, it could be worse. There is a fracture of the fibula that is not displaced, and I suspect that most of the pain and swelling is because you've torn the lateral ligaments. You'll need a plaster cast for about 6 weeks and then some physiotherapy". David responded by opening and closing his mouth like a landed fish before he could think of the most relevant response. "Kareem, as we are now on first name terms, I'm more concerned about my colleagues left behind on our mother ship, Princess Duda. Is there any way you could find out what happened to them in the face of the tsunami?". "Of course, David, go off to our plaster technician and by the time you get back I should have found the answer by searching online on my iMac."

Half an hour later the patient returned with a neatly sculptured plaster cast on his left leg from toes to the knee that was split down the centre to allow for swelling.

As he entered Dr Yacoub's office the expression on the doctor's face told him all he needed to know. "I'm very sorry David but the news is terrible. The coast east of Alexandria has been devastated and the human and material losses have yet to be fully accounted for but I'm afraid, as far anyone can judge amongst this devastation, your ship and all those aboard have been lost."

Dr Goddard bowed over holding his head in his hands, whilst a sense of hopelessness and helplessness overwhelmed him. Meanwhile Dr Yacoub and the two men from the village went into a huddle and engaged in an animated conversation in Arabic.

After about five minutes, Dr Yacoub turned around to address his patient. "David, I understand your despair, locked in the middle of nowhere in a foreign country having lost many friends and worldly goods. You're in no fit state to fly home. We could put you up in a local guest house, but you wouldn't be able to get around on your own. Let me make a suggestion. These good people from the village offer to look after you for at least a week until we replace the split plaster cast with a more solid affair that might allow you to fly home. Before you say anything let me tell you something else. These kind village folk are very superstitious and covertly still venerate the old gods of our ancient ancestors. Finding you amongst the bulrushes on the banks of the Nile, just like the baby Moses, seems to them as if you are a gift from Hapi, Goddess of the Nile. They feel that they have an ethical obligation to take care of you at this time of grief. To offer them money would be judged as an insult. What do you think?". Dr Goddard, thought for a moment or two and slowly lifted his head, and with a wan smile nodded his agreement. "Thank you, Dr Yacoub, tell them I would be honoured, but before I return, I will need to buy some essentials. First of all, I will need a mobile phone, then a pair of jeans, some footwear and underwear and perhaps a 'teach yourself Arabic' book, notebook and pen." There were nods and smiles all around but unknown to the others David Goddard was not going to give up on his find in the depths of the Nile at the ancient archaeological site of Naucratis.

With that, Dr Yacoub said goodbye after arranging a follow-up appointment for one week later, and David supported by the men from the village hopped around the nearby shops.

He found everything he needed except for a "Teach yourself Arabic" handbook.

The drive back was much more comfortable with his leg in plaster but at this point, he was unable to plan his future.

CHAPTER 2

# September the 26th 2019, Central London

A T 16.45, on a balmy autumn evening, Professor Robert Abrahams, accompanied by his statuesque Ethiopian Israelite wife, Sophie, and his strikingly beautiful 16-year-old daughter, Chloe, turned into the gated entry to the quadrangle of University College London (UCL), at the Gower Street entrance. The quad, the cloisters, the neo-classical frontage of the central building, capped with its gleaming white cupola, was made famous by the popular film "Doctor in the House" where it stood in for the fictional St Swithens' Hospital.

UCL was founded in 1826 to open up university education in England to those who had been excluded from it, that included those of a Jewish persuasion. Even more radical than that relaxing of rectitude, in 1878, UCL became the first university in England to admit women students on equal terms with men! No wonder they earned the epithet of "The Godless College of Gower Street". It is therefore of no surprise to learn that its founder was the philosopher and midwife of utilitarianism, Jeremy Bentham.

Professor Abrahams had a spring in his step as he was on his way to deliver his inaugural lecture in the Cavendish lecture theatre on the top floor of the south wing of the main building. A tall and handsome man, with a fashionable three-day stubble on his chin, wearing an unfashionable, ill-fitting dark blue suit. His signature mode of dress, as seen on television, were jeans, a loud check shirt and a yellow V necked sweater. This was often topped with an Indiana Jones style hat, when filming on location at some archaeological dig.

He had just been appointed Professor of Molecular Genealogy at The Centre for Genetic Anthropology (TCGA). His choice of garb for this auspicious event, following a row with his wife who "Wouldn't be seen dead with him in that outfit". His best suit was his only suit that hadn't been worn since his marriage in Jerusalem 17 years ago.

As they walked along the cloisters, the Professor was surprised to note that he was following in the slip stream of a large group of undergraduates and faculty. At the end of the corridor they passed the auto icon of the late, some might say very late, Dr Jeremy Bentham. In a glass fronted mahogany cupboard, he sat dignified on his mahogany chair, in his best clothes, stick in hand and wide brimmed hat, covering his mummified body. Professor Abrahams, stood in front of the old man, and as tradition demanded, bowed in respect. Chloe burst out in a fit of giggles.

They avoided the lifts because of the crush and walked up three sets of stairs to arrive at the lower side door to the auditorium. The receiving party outside was led by the Provost, a very rare honour for the inaugural lecture of a new professor, that were 10 a penny on this sacred ground. But on this occasion, the Provost had succumbed to the celebrity culture of the day, as Professor Abrahams and his super model wife made such a glamorous couple. Sophie and Chloe were led to their reserved seats in the front row, whilst the platform group, the Provost, the faculty Dean and the speaker waited for the audience to settle down. Robert Abrahams was completely relaxed; his PowerPoint presentation had already been loaded up and tested earlier in the day and he enjoyed public speaking if well prepared. At 17.05, the doors were flung open and there was an audible sigh as the speaker was led in. As the Provost embarked on his sonorous introduction, Robert scanned the auditorium to judge the make-up of the audience. The front row was reserved for family and university dignitaries, the next 10 rows were full of faculty members and the 20 back rows filled with undergraduates who spilled down the stairs and stood at the back, all as expected. There was one discordant note though, as he spotted five elderly men wearing black hats and exuberant facial hair. They were of course ultra-orthodox Jews, nowadays referred to as Charedim.

The Provost then ended his introduction with the words; "It is now my pleasure to invite Professor, doctor, doctor, doctor, Abrahams to the lectern to deliver his talk on 'The origins of the Priestly tribe of the ancient

Israelites'". The doctor, doctor, doctor, witticism, was an insider joke to the fact that the speaker had qualified as a medical doctor at Oxford, studied pathology and was awarded a doctorate in molecular genealogy and finally a PhD at the Petrie Institute for Egyptology at UCL. His PhD was awarded for studying traces of DNA in the remnants of bone marrow in mummies from the Petrie Institute or the nearby British Museum.

Just as Professor Abrahams was about to launch his well-prepared talk, he suddenly realised that he wasn't sure of the "pecking order" of the grandees in the first two rows. So, he thought he would make light of it. "Provost, Lord Turnberg, Lady Haversham, Your Grace, Reverend Gentlemen, Colleagues, friends, family and you lowly undergraduates sitting on the stairs who have nowhere to go but upwards in this academic food chain." This brought laughter from the students sitting on the stairs and at a stroke speaker and audience were at their ease. He continued: "To quote Sir Isaac Newton, 'If I can see further than you it is because I'm sitting on the shoulders of a giant'" Nodding to someone in the front row. "Sitting before me is Neil Bradman, founder and chairman of The Centre for Genetic Anthropology. It was him that set me on this path after his seminal discovery of the Cohen model haplotype that confirmed the oral tradition of the lineage of the priesthood in Jewish tradition. Using that as a starting point I want to take you on my voyage of discovery over the last three years that has led to some startling discoveries." Then followed about 15 minutes of methodology and experimentation that was only fully appreciated by the experts in the audience, but was well aware that the undergraduates from the arts faculty and the laymen in the audience would soon get restless, so as planned he switched over the summarise the meaning of his finding and his provocative conclusions.

"So, to sum up the significance of these findings, the extended Y chromosome haplotypes display multiple and unique lineages of the Jewish priesthood. In other words, the detailed dissection of the Y Cohen haplotypes demonstrates correspondence between those amongst the Ashkenazi Cohanim and those amongst the Sephardi and Mizrachi Cohanim. This confirms that the lineage of the priesthood goes back nearly 3,000 years to the fall of the First Temple and the Babylonian exile. In contrast, the opposite is true amongst those Jews whose oral tradition claims they are decedents of the tribe of Levites. There are multiple origins of Ashkenazi Levites with Y Chromosome Evidence for Both Near Eastern and European

Ancestries." Now he had the attention of his audience and there were some rumbling noises coming from the Charedim at the back.

"How can this be? The Cohanim are said to be members of the Levite clan if you accept the Biblical story at its face value. Yet if you dig deeper you find that the Levites were treated as second class citizens. Take this quotation from Numbers 1:47–50

> You must not count the tribe of Levi or include them in the census of the other Israelites. Instead, appoint the Levites to be in charge of the tabernacle of the covenant law—over all its furnishings and everything belonging to it.

So, they were treated as servants rather than Israelites. Furthermore, when the Israelites entered the Promised Land, all tribes were offered parcels of land except for the Levites read how Maimonides explains it at the end of the laws of *Shmitta Vyovel*:

> The entire tribe of Levi are commanded against receiving an inheritance in the land of Canaan, and they were commanded against receiving a share in the spoil when the cities are conquered, as Deuteronomy states: "The priest and the Levites—the entire tribe of Levi—should not have a portion and an inheritance among Israel." "A portion of the spoil; refers to a portion of the land. And as stated in Numbers 18:20: "You shall not receive a heritage in their land, nor will you have a portion among them," If a Levite takes a portion of the spoil, he is punished by lashes

So, Ladies and Gentlemen, if the Cohanim are not of the tribe of Levites then where do they come from? I have no idea, but I'm determined to find out!

There was a pause and then the audience burst out in applause and foot stamping, even the students sitting on the steps stood up to clap. After the noise had died down, the Dean of the faculty, Dr Ambrose Goodenough, asked for questions. There was an expectant silence until a booming voice from the back row of bearded men broke the peace. "Young man, my name is Rabbi Moishe Ben Levy. As my name suggests, I am proud to be a Levite. Are you trying to disinherit my tribe are you even saying I'm not really a Jew at all! Throughout the Torah, the Levites were venerated as custodians of the Temple and Moses was our leader until Joshua took us into the Promised Land. You are guilty of heresy and my brethren and I have agreed to pronounce a curse on you and all your family and to excommunicate you from amongst the chosen of Hashem!" There was an immediate uproar in the lecture theatre with booing and catcalling directed at the black hats. It took a while for the Provost to regain order. He turned to the speaker and spoke in a whisper; "Professor Abrahams, I'm really sorry about this, would you like the last word?" Robert was seething with fury but was able to control himself and end with the following words. "Rabbi Levy, you misconstrued what I said. The Levites have 3,000 years of acceptance as Jews and many like you have become great leaders of our communities. You may have had humble beginnings but then so have I and most of the people in this room be they Jews or Non-Jews. Whilst your ancestors were serving in King Solomon's Temple our Provost's ancestors were probably painting themselves in wode. Yet you can't have it both ways, you celebrated Bradman's discovery of the Cohen model haplotype, yet you curse my findings using the same techniques. I reject your curse and your accusation of heresy; it is the last resort of the intellectually bankrupt."

Pandemonium broke out and Professor Abrahams and his family were ushered out through the lower side door and guided to comfort and safety in the senior common room were a drinks and snacks reception had been set out.

CHAPTER 3

# SEPTEMBER THE 20ᵀᴴ 2019, STAMFORD HILL, NORTH LONDON

T o the average gentile in the United Kingdom, if asked what they know about Jews, the first thing that springs to mind is the image of an old man, with a long black beard, a black hat and a long black coat. The fact that playwright Tom Stoppard or the TV presenter Emily Maitlis are Jewish, doesn't really fit the stereotype. This is not out of malice but simply that some subgroups of Jews where their faith upon their sleeves; literally as well as figuratively.

These men in black hats, followed by women in modest clothing wearing turbans over their wigs whilst juggling children of ages ranging from neonates to young teenagers, used to be called Chassidim but are now lumped together as Charedim with the Chassidim now relegated to a subset in the taxonomy orthodox Jewry. Yet the word orthodoxy is hardly sufficient to understand these sects. Some men attending orthodox synagogues consider it reasonable to watch Spurs if they are playing at home on Shabbat, providing, they have a season ticket and don't have to carry money, whilst at the other extreme some groups believe that Moses didn't go far enough. For some reason they are referred to as left wing or right wing. In politics we understand what this means. Left wing believes in nationalisation of industries and that Stalin at least freed the serfs, whereas right wing believes the freedom to rob the poor for the benefit of the rich and that the Nazis at least got the trains to run on time. It's better to think of these Jewish sects as more or less fundamentalist. This way the index of

14

extremism swings from those who look upon the Talmud and the Torah as a good guide for living your life unless it clashes with other categorical imperatives (viz. Spurs playing at home on the Sabbath) all the other way to keeping every minutia of the laws for human behaviour whilst searching and interpreting every linguistic clue for making life more difficult for their women and children. These groups are in a hurry for the Messiah to come and believe that their rituals will hasten his arrival.

All these sects are closed communities with a hereditary leader known as the *Rebbe*.

There are subtle details in their mode of dress that defines these communities, that date back to those that were fashionable in the villages and towns of the mid 19thC eastern Europe where the first *Rebbe* held court. Some tuck their trousers in their socks, some don't. Some wear black socks and some wear white socks. On *Shabbat* some wear tall fur hats and some wear bagel shaped hats. As far as the women are concerned, as long as their arms are covered, their hair is covered, the skirt is 12 inches above their ankles and their ankles are covered in black woollen tights, they can wear anything they like.

Reb Moishe Ben Levy belonged to the Shabbatai Zevi sect. They are one of the largest Chasidic dynasties in the world: The estimated number of affiliated men, women, and children ranges between 65,000 and 75,000. It is characterized by extremely strict religious adherence, complete rejection of modern culture, and fierce anti-Zionism. Within Shabbatai Zevi there are those who align themselves with the Temple Mount Faithful Movement, whose goal is to rebuild the Third Jewish Temple on the Temple Mount in Jerusalem and re-institute the practice of ritual sacrifice. Only then would the Messiah come, and the State of Israel would be a theocracy ruled by the faithful. The assassination of Yitzhak Rabin on 4th November 1995 by Yigal Amir, illustrates just how far their warped philosophy might lead to, if anyone tried to impede them in their Messianic mission.

Moishe Ben Levy, finished leading the morning prayers in his *shtiebel* (house of prayer) at 8.00am and as the congregation of 12 where removing their *tallis* and *tefillin*, he summoned his most trusted group of followers, those who had witnessed the blasphemy at UCL the previous evening, for a "war council" in his private office. The house of prayers was no more than one barren room with a wooden flour and a collection of ill matched folding chairs. The walls were free of decoration apart from an ancient mahogany cupboard, hung on the wall, that held their treasured *sefer torah*, that had been rescued on *Kristallnacht* November 10th, 1938, from the burning remains of one of the old synagogues in Mainz, by his grandfather.

The *shtiebel* was to be found up a steep set of stairs above a dry cleaners' shop, on Stoke Newington High Street.

"My brothers, what we heard last night was not only an abomination and a blasphemy, but a threat to disenfranchise the tribe of the Levites. Should these false facts gain traction, then our whole mission to lead the fight for the building of the Third Temple and the coming of the Messiah, could be in jeopardy. What are we to do about?".

The first to answer was, Reb Nahchum Ben Eliezer, Hacohen, the oldest member of the group, an 89-year-old, grey bearded, bent-over bigot. His words embodied Ogden Nash's aphorism.

> The door of a bigoted mind opens outwards so that the only result of the pressure of facts upon it is to close it more snugly.

He started his words in Hebrew from the Yom Kippur prayer that warns of the punishments that may follow your sins.

> *And for the sins for which we incur the penalty of lashing for rebelliousness. And for the sins for which we incur the penalty of forty lashes. And for the sins for which we incur the penalty of death by the hand of Heaven. And for the sins for which we incur the penalty of excision and childlessness. And for the sins for which we incur the penalty of the four forms of capital punishment executed by the Court: stoning, burning, decapitation and strangulation.*

The others, on balance, thought these punishments were a bit premature and a bit of an over-reaction. They debated back and forth until the youngest of the group, Joshua Ben Moishe Levy, the son of their leader came up with a brilliantly simple solution. This involved formidable skills in Information Technology (IT), the last thing you would have expected from these mediaevalists. The secret here was that they lived lives according to the teachings of a mid 19thC Rabbi yet funded these lives for all their co-religionists, by controlling the diamond bourses in Antwerp, Tel Aviv, Manhattan and Hatton Garden London. For this they had to develop algorithms that monitored the flux in prices of raw and cut diamonds appearing on the market by fair means or foul, adjust their paper-thin margins and set their prices. As brokers, getting a few minutes lead over your competitors might accrue a $10,000 profit or loss. Young Joshua had mastered these skills and suggested his team cyberattack Professor Abrahams' computer, find the relevant files, tamper with the numbers in his results, then find a willing colleague to accuse him of scientific conduct. All he needed was an insider who was sufficiently knowledgeable to understand the science and come up with plausible forgeries. Such an accomplice would either be someone sympathetic to their cause or a lab technician with a grudge and a large hole in his wallet. $10,000 would be more than enough to win the support of such a man.

The room went silent as they all started thinking of the flaws in the proposal until Joshua's father broke the silence. "This is a brilliant suggestion but how would you even find such a person willing to risk his reputation and future in his scientific career." "That Abba, is the tricky bit, hacking his hard drive is easy, we do it all the time, but recruiting an accomplice requires profiling. We start by building a psychological profile on the person we have in mind and take it step by step using this kind of algorithm. First, we look for someone with a grievance; he is over-qualified for the job and/or overlooked at the last round of promotions. In this specific case, we might search his Twitter account to see if has exhibited anti-Semitic or anti-Zionist tendencies. We may fail at this first level and have to start again, but assuming we have one or more candidates, we find their addresses and judge their circumstances by the address code, to state the exterior of the house and the car they're driving. Two or more children or a wife with expensive tastes, might then confirm that we have locked down on a vulnerable target. In the meantime, one of you might contact our brethren at the Shaare Zedek Medical Centre, in Jerusalem, or *Bnei Brak's Mayanei Hayeshua* Medical Centre, to see if they will collaborate with us by coming up with another set of data of their own and then accuse Professor Abrahams of falsifying his results. They all agreed that it was a long shot but worth the effort whilst keeping stoning, burning, decapitation and strangulation in reserve.

Robert Abrahams' laboratories were on the top of the Rockefeller building, a red brick Edwardian monstrosity on University street that was overshadowed by the neo-classical building of the original campus. The building had no obvious internal structure but consisted of a rabbit warren of corridors and undersized rooms created at the whim of generations of newly appointed professors who knew nothing about interior design. The top floor was reached by a side entrance on Huntley street and served by an open caged antique lift. Like most clinical academics, Abrahams cared nothing about computer security and left it to his chief technician, George

Skanderbeg PhD, an Albanian with a chip on his shoulder. He hadn't appointed him but more or less inherited him from the previous director of these laboratories. He tried to get replaced, but Dr Skanderbeg was a bit of a "barrack-room lawyer" and knew his rights under the unfair dismissal clause of the British employment laws. He came to Britain in 1992 seeking entry as a fugitive from Kosovo. At that time, he was 25 with a BSc in chemistry and saw himself as a rising star. This opinion was not shared by his colleagues and took him 5 more years before he submitted his thesis on molecular biology and was awarded a PhD in 1997 at the Welsh National School of Medicine in Cardiff. At the age of 32 he was successful in being appointed as a senior laboratory technician at UCL but the contrast in House prices between London and Cardiff left him with a huge mortgage that was only made affordable by sending his new wife, a pretty Welsh girl named Bronwyn (Welsh for fair breasts), out to work as a waitress in a nearby hotel. Now at the age of 52, with two children, a second mortgage and a glamorous wife, he was both desperate and angry with the society that had treated him so badly. Just as chance favours the brave and luck follows those with a prepared mind, Joshua Ben Moishe Levy, had no difficulty tracking down Dr Skanderberg, and had no difficulty of recruiting him to their cause. Their deception worked without a hitch and two months later, Robert Abrahams was summoned to Dean Goodenough's office to learn that he was suspended from his post pending investigation of the accusation of scientific misconduct would he kindly hand over his UCL identity tag plus the touch card for entry to the Rockefeller building.

# CHAPTER 4

# FRIDAY, NOVEMBER THE 8ᵀᴴ, 2019, CAIRO, EGYPT

P ROFESSOR Abdul Sharif, aged 72, was the Professor of anatomy and paleopathology at Cairo University. The medical faculty of the University was at Casir el-Einy, where the great Mameluke Palace was built in 1467 by Ahmed Ibn el-Einy whose tomb, was part of the site. The Palace was used as the official residence of the Turkish viceroys of Egypt until the French invasion of 1798; Napoleon held his council of war there the night before the battle of the pyramids and it was later turned into a military hospital. In 1890 it became the medical school occupying new premises built on the site by the British administration, that somehow spoilt the exotic exterior of the old building. His office, however, was in the original building with views looking south towards the pyramids at Giza. He had a town house in a fashionable quarter of the city nearby but preferred his weekend retreat close to the step pyramid of Djoser at Saqqara. Three walls of his office carried floor to ceiling teak bookshelves from the days of the Ottoman Empire, that were filled with his collection of specimen jars of mummified organs from canopic jars, his personal collection of ancient Egyptian scarabs and signet rings and his pride and joy, the mummified right index finger of Pharaoh, Amenhotep III, a gift from the director of antiquities, his cousin, Zahi Awass. Abdul Sharif likes to play the role of the silver fox in front of his beautiful lady undergraduates. In many ways he looked like his namesake, Omar Sharif, with close-cropped grey hair, a military-looking grey moustache and beautiful white teeth, with one exception; his stocky build. To compensate for that he always wore immac-ulately tailored suits when teaching in the anatomy department or chairing a committee. His claim to fame was the discovery of the human remains of those workers who had actually built the pyramids at Giza, when he was a young PhD student in the early 1980s. The cemetery he discovered revealed that they had not been slaves, but a core workforce whose numbers were swelled by farmers, temporarily redeployed for this huge and ambitious project for three months every year when their fields were submerged by the Nile Flood.

He was sitting in his office in a sombre mood, having spent the last week dealing with the aftermath of the tsunami that wreaked so much car-nage on the coastline east of Alexandria. He had lost two colleagues and one of his PhD students following the destruction of the mother ship of the underwater excavations of Thonis-Haracleion. Out of respect, an im-portant conference at the Medical School in Alexandria had been cancelled and as chairman of the conference organisation, he carried responsibility for advising all the foreign faculty and start thinking of how they could reconvene the meeting sometime next year.

He cheered up a little on realising it was Friday and that meant he would soon be sharing the weekend with his wife and some of his grand-children in his second home.

Professor Sharif has five children, two were doctors in his own institu-tion, and 12 grandchildren. He was in the process of organising a 50th wed-ding anniversary for December that year. Although enjoying the company of beautiful young women, he had always been faithful to his beloved wife, Fatima.

The party was to take place over two days in the compound of his week-end retreat and as well as his extended family he intended to invite some of his favourite colleagues from abroad. The compound close to Saqqara step pyramid, was in itself an important archaeological site. The Saqqara pyramid is much older than its famous neighbours at Giza. It was built in the 27th century BC during the Third Dynasty for the burial of Pharaoh Djoser. The pyramid is the central feature of a vast mortuary complex in an enormous courtyard surrounded by ceremonial structures and decoration. Outside this major courtyard there are a number of other walled off rect-angles that were thought to home the builders of the edifice. One of these, thought to be of little scientific interest, was purchased 20 years earlier by Professor Sharif, with permission of the director of antiquities at that time who accepted a modest token sum of backsheesh to help with the transaction. The original 5,000-year-old walls had mostly crumbled into dust but sometime during the 18thC a Turkish landowner had raised the walls and used the enclosure for his flock of sheep. Whilst clearing the ground for building his weekend retreat, his workmen uncovered bones and artefacts that confirmed the area had been used as a little village for the builders of the pyramid. He began with a modest mud brick single-story bungalow but step by step, over the years, this had been replaced by a modernist looking two-story mansion with a flat roof, mimicking the appearance of a home of an important member of an 18th dynasty Pharaoh's, household. Further bungalows for visiting guests and to house his staff, were built. There was also an outdoor kitchen with a traditional oven for baking flatbread and a spit over a fire pit to barbeque the odd goat or two. They then employed a traditional douser, who by fair means or foul, discovered a fresh water supply 10 metres below the surface, that provided a well with a steady supply of fresh water. By the time of the dawning of the new millennium, Abdul Sharif had recreated a village of his forefathers equipped with all mod cons, that included air conditioning and Wi-Fi, with electricity supplied by a powerful generator outside the western wall. As the family had increased in size over the last year or two, he recruited a firm of architects and builders, to construct an annexe as a lean-to, against the back of the mansion just outside the original walls of the compound. He was pushing them hard to have it completed in time for his Golden wedding party. One can imagine his dismay, when the foreman at the site, phoned with the news that they had just discovered a sarcophagus in the pit they were excavating under the toilet for the new annexe. His first question was whether the box was made from wood or granite. If the latter then the department of antiquities would have to be informed, as the mummies in their coffins, inside might be from high ranking officers of the Royal Household, whilst wooden might only contain the humble copses of workers. Once the antiquities department was involved, the bureaucracy might hold up the completion of the works.

He was somewhat relieved to learn that the foreman thought it was dark wood.

Professor Sharif cancelled all the remaining appointments in his schedule, jumped into his silver E class Mercedes parked just by the main entrance, and raced in a southerly direction towards Saqqara.

As soon as he got to his weekend retreat, he rushed in a changed into his khaki jumpsuit, and with a perfunctory kiss on startled wife's cheek, rushed round the back of the summer house.

Anthony and Cleopatra, his two camels that were kept in a paddock for the entertainment of his grandchildren and their friends, then trotted over to see why their master had come home so early. Ignoring their kisses of welcome, he found his way to the edge of the pit where his foreman, Mohamed El Masri, was waiting. The pit was about two metres deep and at the bottom he could see clearly in the noon day sun, a dark brown box measuring about 2 X 6 metres. It looked like cedar wood but its corners and edges, were heavily coated in black bitumen, made it difficult to be sure. To his relief, they looked very much like the workers' sarcophagi he had unearthed at Giza, but he had no recall of seeing as specimen like this in the necropolis at Saqqara. Out of respect for the dead and a large dose of curiosity, he instructed his workmen to pull it out from its resting place. That was no easy job and required the them to drive over their mechanical hoist and find some heavy-duty chains to slip under the base of the wooden box. This had to be done slowly and gently because for all he could see, hidden under the rock-hard aged bitumen, some of the wood might have turned to dust. Whilst they were gathering their kit, Professor Sharif strolled back to his country villa to explain to his wife why he was home so early. As it was Friday, his wife had arrived well ahead of the master of the house in order to chivvy her staff to make everything nice for the weekend.

He was offered a cold glass of lemonade and rested under the shade of a banana tree by the front door whilst describing his first impressions of the find.

About an hour later, the Professor was invited back to the building site followed by a curious retinue made up of Fatima, Anthony and Cleopatra. The chains under the box were now in place, running across its length and breadth, linked to chains at each corner gathered up to a focal point in the claw on the arm of the mechanical hoist. At the order of Sharif, the ancient sarcophagus was lifted inch by inch and just at the point when it was to be swung to the side, there was a loud sound of splintering wood, and three mummies fell out a crashed down to the bottom of the pit. Fatima and Cleopatra screamed so loudly as to drown out the shouts of profanity from the master of the house.

Once the clamour had died down and the camels had been returned to their paddock, Prof Sharif too stock of the situation. He wasn't that worried about the ancient wooden sarcophagus, they were not that rare and searching for its historical provenance could wait, but he was very upset that the mummies might have been damaged by falling back into the pit from a height of about two metres. He asked everyone to stay put, for fear that someone's curiosity might end up by falling on top of the mummies. He walked slowly to the edge of the pit and then peered over the edge. He was somewhat reassured to see that all three mummies had landed on their backs and remained intact as far as he could see. On further inspection, lit by the fierce midday sun, the shorter of the three was encapsulated in, what from his viewpoint, looked like a papier-mâché coffin.

The elite amongst the dead of ancient Egypt were buried in coffin sets based on the same principle as Russian nested matryoshka dolls, where objects are nested inside each other to constitute a complete ensemble. For example, Tutankhamun was buried in as many as eight coffins. For men and women who were members of the Royal household at that time, three or four coffins were not unusual.

Nested coffins were not only a status symbol for the Egyptian elite, but they also played a key role in the process that would link the deceased to their ancestors as well Osiris, the god of the afterlife, and to Amun-Ra, the sun- and creator god.

The numerous layers of coffins around the mummy functioned as repeated images of the deceased, but also as protective capsules, similar to the larvae's pupa before its transformation to a butterfly. In the Egyptian coffin sets, they symbolize the eternal life-giving pendulum of the sun god between heaven and earth—a process in which the ancient Egyptians hoped to participate in their afterlife.

The innermost layer was the most important one, since it shows the objective of the afterlife transformation: the "state of paradise" to which these people aspired involved not only a mystical union with the gods; but more importantly a return to their old *Ka*.

You might think that a papier-mâché coffin suggested that the corpse inside came from a humble background, but that is not the case. The material itself wasn't simple paper and backing powder, but a much more complex recipe that included rare resins and gum-based aromatic material. If the deceased was a woman, some of these castes flattered the female form and were often beautifully decorated with pictures of the dead going about her daily chores or sitting with her husband and playing with her children. Finally having a papier-mâché case for the deceased linen-wrapped body, making it easier for the artisans to start building the outer coffins in wood and more precious materials. From the lip of the pit, the doll shaped figure looked as if her carapace was densely covered with marks that had faded over at least three millennia. She, assuming it was a woman, might have been of some importance and that the innermost coffin had been removed to be interred away from its original burying site, a common practice after the original tomb had been raided by thieves from ancient times.

The other two mummies of manly build, in contrast, looked as if they were wrapped in a hurry. Professor Sharif found this all very intriguing and argued with himself whether or not to let his cousin, the head of the department of antiquities know about this extraordinary find.

He put that decision aside for a moment and re-examined the fractured wooden sarcophagus.

It did not belong to the era of the Saqqara necropolis but more like the ones he had unearthed at Giza. This suggested that the wooden box waiting for future clients *en route* to the afterlife had been stolen and carried 27 Km south to its last resting place. Unlikely, but all sorts of unlikely and bizarre behaviour traits of the ancient Egyptians, were the burden of the modern Egyptologist.

He then turned his attention again to the mummies and sent two men down steep wooden stepladders who gently shifted the mummies, one by one onto hammocks, to be pulled up to the surface.

The papier-mâché coffin was so beautifully constructed that it looked like ceramic. There were no joints to be seen and at one time it must have been covered with painted works of art.

All that could be recognised as the ghost of a cartouche near the feet, and hints of other ancient Egyptian motives, like Ankh crosses, the head of Anubis, traces of what might have figures and the hint of a smile on the face. From what little there was to see, it appeared to be from the 18th Dynasty. The other two corpses had been so rapidly and carelessly wrapped, that the parchment-like skin was glimpsed between the wraps of linen of the larger of the two.

The Professor then had the corpses lifted onto trestle tables for closer inspection. He played little attention to what he assumed to be the poorly wrapped cadavers of humble status but was hypnotised by the elegantly beautiful coffin that look like porcelain. He simply couldn't make sense of this ensemble. He would need a group of expert Egyptologists to help him solve the mystery of the porcelain coffin and its companions, and that would take some time to assemble. A brilliant idea then sprang to mind. Such an assembly had already been summoned, and first amongst equals was his cousin Zahi Awass director of antiquities. The group of foreign Egyptologists included a brilliant expert on molecular genealogy, Prof Robert Abrahams, from University College London, with his beautiful Nubian wife, Sophie. In addition, his partner on many expeditions, Lucy Carpenter, was expected. She was a world authority on ancient Egyptian fabric, hair styles and wigs, whose domicile was in Leeds but who spent most of her life touring the world as a consultant for identifying the dates in which mummies had lived prior to the afterlife. They were all expected to attend his Golden Wedding on December the 20th and could enjoy no better entertainment than unwrapping mummies leaving the Professor and his wife to unwrap their presents. So, for now he would store them in an outhouse he had built that had a thermostat to control the temperature. Humidity was not a problem in this part of the world.

The three "unexpected guests" at the party would not only guarantee its success but was also a cunning plan for avoiding delays thanks to the paperwork demanded by the Egyptian department of antiquities.

# CHAPTER 5

# DECEMBER 1ˢᵀ, 2019, UCL

H ow University College London established the world's first academic centre for Egyptology is a story by itself, going back to the days of expansionism of the British Empire in the mid 19thC. Egypt was occupied by the British as a result of the Anglo-Egyptian war in 1882.

The first period of British rule until the start of World War 1, is often called the "veiled protectorate". During this time Egypt remained an autonomous province of the Ottoman Empire and the British occupation had no legal basis but constituted a *de facto* protectorate over the country. Egypt was thus not part of the British Empire. This state of affairs lasted until 1914 when the Ottoman Empire joined the war on the side of Germany and Britain declared a protectorate over Egypt.

The period of the "veiled protectorate" witnessed the blossoming of Egyptology that was popularised by the authoress, Amelia Edwards. She was one of those indomitable Victorian women who were not impeded by heavy crinoline garments in their eagerness to explore the far-flung countries of the Empire upon which the sun never set. Her most famous book, an Egyptian travelogue *A Thousand Miles up the Nile* (1875), sold thousands of copies and the picture of her riding a camel in front of the Sphinx on the title page, became an icon of the age. During that voyage Edwards was accompanied by her friend Lucy Renshawe. They travelled southwards from Cairo in a hired dahabiyeh house-boat, visiting Philae and ultimately reached Abu Simbel, where they remained for six weeks.

Edwards' travels in Egypt made her aware of increasing threats to ancient monuments from tourism and modern development. She set out to hinder these through public awareness and scientific endeavour, becoming an advocate for research and preservation of them. In 1882, she co-founded the Egypt Exploration Fund. Amelia Edwards was pivotal in securing hundreds of pounds for the fund through writing popular articles about the discoveries, thousands of letters, and talks around the world. Her enthusiasm and determination to preserve the past helped young archaeologists get out to Egypt to study the sites as they should have been. The careers of many were furthered by this opportunity, including that of the young Flinders Petrie who was meticulous, determined and passionate about his work. Seeing the promise in Petrie, Amelia wanted him to have a university Chair — ensuring both the employment of Petrie, and the continuing study of Egyptology in the UK. The Edwards Chair at UCL would be the first in England but had to await her death. Her collections, library and £5000 were left to UCL. This sum together with her collection of objects from ancient Egypt were the foundation stones for the Flinders Petrie museum we can see today, and for Egyptology as an academic subject.

Flinders Petrie was an extraordinary man with astonishing energy and invention. He discovered and began the exploration of many of the famous archaeological sites linked to the names of the great Pharaonic dynasties. One of his protegees, Howard Carter, went on to discover the tomb of Tutankhamun in 1922.

He single-handed invented a taxonomy of ancient pottery ostraca to help the dating of any new site. He collected hundreds of skeletal remains and shipped them back to his colleagues at UCL and the nearby British Museum. One of their tasks was to measure the volume of the cranium to help him come up with another taxonomy, that was used to judge the intelligence of the tribes, slaves and the elite along the length of the river Nile valley. He achieved great distinction, was elected FRS and was knighted in 1923.

However, there was a very dark side to his character. He had a very high opinion of himself and believed he was a prime example of the evolutionary peak of *homo sapiens*. He was a racist and a eugenicist. He believed that at the bottom of the league of human evolution were the negroes and just above them, second from the bottom were the Jews. He was in collusion with Francis Galton, founder of the eugenic movement and Karl Pearson, the statistician, who was the first professor of eugenics at UCL. Pearson's role was to provide statistical proof that the cranial volumes of the negroes and the Jews were significantly smaller than the northern Aryan races. Karl Pearson was awarded a doctorate from the University of Berlin, which was the petri dish for the incubation of Hitler's Nazi racist movement.

Petrie died in Jerusalem in 1942 yet his head was bequeathed to the Royal College of Surgeons in his vainglorious belief, that was an exemplar of the Aryan race. Hubris precedes nemesis and this case, black comedy.

All of this story only reached public awareness following the publication of the book by Debbie Challis, *The archaeology of race: The eugenic idea of Francis Galton and Flinders Petrie,* in 2013. This was a huge embarrassment to UCL. After 5 years of wrangling the Provost set up an independent board of enquiry that published their findings in 2019.

Lucy Carpenter was a member of this board.

Lucy was a child of the "Windrush generation" carried in her mother's arms, arriving in the UK, from Barbados in 1960. She was now a Professor of Egyptology at Leeds University.

Her father, Winston Carpenter, fought in the Caribbean Regiment as a unit of the British Army during World War II. The regiment was overseas in July 1944 and he saw service in the Middle East and Italy. There had been resistance from the War Office to forming the West Indian Regiment, but those who made their own way to the UK were able to enlist in the British Army. Winston was one of nearly 10,000 West Indians who travelled and joined the army in Britain. He reached the rank of sergeant and was mentioned in dispatches for his gallantry. Like many of his kind, he found that the post-war West Indies offered few chances for making a comfortable living and jumped at the opportunity provided by the British Government, to be welcome as an immigrant. Welcomed, they were not. Lucy remembered her father's stories about their early years in London when seeking rooms to rent. Most of the properties in the more gentrified areas of the city, carried cards in their windows reading "No dogs or blacks". The racism was ubiquitous, and the unionised trades would always prefer the white man to the black man when seeking employment or promotion. In the end, he settled in Brixton, a very poor and violent corner of southeast London and set up a fruit stall in the Cold Harbour Lane open-air market. He had made a smart decision to import exotic fruit from the Caribbean islands, just at the time of a long post-war period of austerity had come to an end, and just when the emerging middle class had sufficient money to broaden their tastes. It was considered trendy to take the Northern line on the tube to this dark and scary district and bring home a pineapple and a mango. It was as close to a safari as they could afford.

Mr and Mrs Carpenter, working side by side at their market stall, were a very popular couple and built of a regular clientele. They were then able to put down a deposit to buy a two up two down terrace house at the "smart" end of Cold Harbour lane close by Kings College Hospital, were Lucy's brother, Emanuel was born.

They could not afford a private school for Lucy but she was a very bright girl and won a scholarship at Archbishop Tenison's School, near the Kennington, Oval. Her father was delighted for two reasons, first that his daughter would stand a better chance in life than he had and secondly because the Oval was the home of the Surrey County Cricket Club.

Winston was a fanatic about the game and could bowl a googly as good as any English County white flannelled snob. The happiest days of his life were in the late 1970s when West Indies greatest cricket dynasty went 15 years without losing a test series. To watch England's finest humiliated on the Oval ground by the "Windies", made up in part the racism he suffered during his early years in the UK.

Lucy grew up to be a statuesque beauty who wore her hair short only to accentuate her long neck. She studied hard and achieved the highest marks in her class at the GSE and A level exams in her class. Her favourite subjects were history and mathematics. Her obvious choice for a University education was the very liberal University College London, where the fact that she was black and of the female gender, went unnoticed. She won a state scholarship and took up her place at the Institute of Archaeology in 1978. It was not long before her lifetime interest in Egyptology was ignited following a visit to the Petrie Museum on campus. Three years later having been granted a BA with distinction she registered for a PhD and her tutor, Harry Smith, thought it might be ladylike to pursue research in women's costumes and hairstyles.

At first, she thought Prof Smith was patronising her, but she then saw that there was a mischievous twinkle in his eye. He went on to explain that from the time of Flinders Petrie until the present, there was extreme difficulty in determining the sex of an individual, either from cartouche, painted hieroglyphics, or friezes carved on the walls of temples and palaces or even a mummy. This even applied to the identity of Pharaohs, some of whom turned out to be women. There were no obvious separate words for he and she, men and women both wore kilts, and both wore wigs. Furthermore, statues of Pharaohs were often androgynous in appearance as part of the mysterious concepts of ancient Egyptian polytheism.

He went on to suggest she spent the first and third year of her studies on campus and the middle year at the temple of Aten at Tell-el-Amarna, that had originally been discovered and identified by Flinders Petrie in 1890. There she would be in the safe hands of his old friend Professor Sharif, from the University of Cairo.

Her studies went very well, and her thesis was entitled, "Akhenaten and Nefertiti: Joint regents illustrating the male/female nexus in Ancient Egyptian mysticism", was very well received and ultimately published as a book.

For that reason, she was forever grateful to the legendary Flinders Petrie, who discovered the ruins of the Temple and provided much material and a number of mummies for her to study in the Petrie Museum, of the British Museum in nearby Bloomsbury.

Whilst in Egypt she met her future husband, Angus McCartney and they both ended up as Professors in Leeds, another male/female duality.

From this résumé, she was obviously a shoe-in as a member of the UCL board of enquiry. On the one hand her family had suffered from racism yet on the other hand you couldn't simply ignore Flinders Petrie's contribution to her subject; "*autres temps, autres mœurs.*" The Board of enquiry, chaired by Professor Iyiola Solanke, of the University of Leeds, started their work in 2018 and completed their report in September 2019, with their findings shared with the general public on the 28th of February. This is a redacted version of the press release.

UCL is today announcing a range of measures aimed at acknowledging and addressing the university's historical links with the eugenics movement.

*These include funding new scholarships to study race and racism, a commitment to ensure UCL staff and students learn about the history and legacy of eugenics and the creation of a two-year research post to further examine UCL's history of eugenics.*

*UCL President & Provost will also recommend that the university's 'Buildings Naming and Renaming Committee' start the formal process of considering the current naming of spaces and buildings after two prominent eugenicists Francis Galton and Karl Pearson.*

*Victorian scientist Francis Galton coined the term eugenics and en-*
*dowed UCL with his personal collection and archive along with a*
*bequest for the country's first professorial Chair of Eugenics.*

*The panel of prominent UCL academics and equality repre-*
*sentatives from UCL and the Students' Union spent more than a*
*year examining UCL's historical role in and the current status of the*
*teaching and study of eugenics as well as any financial instruments*
*linked to the study of eugenics which may benefit the institution. It*
*undertook archival research as well as a survey of attitudes towards*
*eugenics inside and outside the UCL community.*

*The Inquiry recommends that UCL acknowledges and addresses*
*the university's historical links with eugenics in a wide range of areas*
*including the teaching, dissemination and study of eugenics.*

Shortly after the Board's work was done in September 2019, Lucy had
an e-mail from her old mentor, Professor Sharif in Cairo, inviting her and
her husband to a Golden wedding party in December and to please stay
over for the Christmas, New Year period. The thought of a couple of weeks
holiday in a sunny climate outside the University term, was too great a
temptation to reject. Professor McCartney, professor of ancient Egyptian
languages, hastened to endorse that decision.

CHAPTER 6

# DECEMBER 20ᵀᴴ, 2019, SAQQARA

PROFESSOR Robert Abrahams, accompanied by Sophie, boarded the early morning EgyptAir flight from London Heathrow bound for Cairo, at 8.00 am. They left their 16-year-old daughter, Chloe, behind who insisted on spending the Christmas holidays with her boyfriend's family in Stanmore, who had a huge house with an indoor pool and cinema room. All her classmates had planned a big party there and she hadn't the slightest interest in ancient old Egyptian mummies and daddies. There was a bit of a screaming match at first but in the end, her parents were somewhat relieved as they were a little concerned about security for her if left alone whilst they explored some of the nearby archaeological sites. On reaching the door of the 747 they were delighted to be invited to turn left as someone of importance in Egypt had arranged for them to be upgraded to business class. The same good fortune was handed out to Professors McCartney and Carpenter, who boarded the plane shortly afterwards. The foursome found themselves seated on either side of the aisle in seats, 4 A to 4 D. It didn't take more than a few exchanges of pleasantries to learn that they were off to the same house parties. They hit it off immediately and remained in animated conversation for most of the 8-hour flight. Although Sophie Abrahams had a limited knowledge of Egyptology and was in danger of being left out of the conversation, it soon became apparent that Angus McCartney was captivated by her exotic beauty and even flattered her by saying she reminded him of Angelina Jolie. Robert turned to Sophie who was sitting in the window seat and gave his wife a wink. Thereafter the conversation changed direction so that could all share their life histories. By the time they disembarked at the Cairo International airport they felt they knew each other like favourite cousins.

They were treated as VIPs as they walked through passport control and baggage retrieval.

Waiting in front of the arrivals exit, was an illegally parked large black shiny Mercedes people mover, and in less than 45 minutes from touch down they were travelling south out of Cairo, on the edge of the desert, on the way to Saqqara. Lucy knew the area very well having spent 12 months in the vicinity, but Robert had been here only once and that visit ended up with a disaster. On his first visit to Egypt 5 years earlier, he was speaking at an international conference in Cairo and was befriended by Professor Sharif, who invited him to spend the weekend with him and his family in their country retreat. He was thrilled by the invitation and the family made a big fuss over him. They roasted a goat on the BBQ and Professor Sharif was liberal with his wine collection, in spite of his religious beliefs. After dinner he offered a fine malt whiskey in a highball glass "on the rocks" in the American style. Robert had been warned in advance of the threat of "the curse of the Pharaohs," if he drank any water from municipal sources. When he hesitated to accept the drink expressing his concern, the old Professor feigned righteous indignation, "Professor Abrahams, my water is pure, it comes from my own well that is fed by an underground source draining off the mountains to the west". What could he do? To refuse would appear to be churlish. So, he accepted the whiskey graciously, and 6 hours later the bacterial toxins hit the mucosa of the caecum and ascending co-lon. He then spent the night and the next 24 hours running backwards and forwards to the men's room.

They arrived at Saqqara as the sun was setting behind the great step pyramid. The view was spectacular as the pyramid was viewed in silhouette against a background of orange, indigo and violet, with not a cloud to break up the view. The greeting party at the gateway to the compound was led by Professor Sharif and his beaming wife. They were backed by about a dozen saucer-eyed children ranging from about 7 to 17. In addition, there was a servant to collect their luggage, barking dogs, two curious camels and one unfortunate goat that was to be lunch the following day. The four guests were warmly embraced by their hosts and led off to their accommodation. The plan was for them to freshen up, change their clothes and meet up for drinks at the outdoor bar next to the clay oven. By that time, it was after 8.00 pm, and the guests were tired but excited by the prospect of spending a few days in this delightful oasis in the sands of time. All four guests had elected to wear fashionable safari suits in shades of khaki, with Sophie Abrahams wearing shorts that exposed a long length of shapely leg.

The two women accepted glasses of gin and tonic with ice and lime. The men settled for malt whiskey and when Robert was asked if he would like it on the rocks, he went a shade of pale, not obvious against the purple sky. Professor Sharif hastened to reassure them that the water supplies were now fitted with filters and charcoal that took care of both bacteria and toxins. The children were sent off to bed and the adults, now joined by two of the Sharif's sons and their wives, settled down under some date palms to enjoy their drinks, accompanied by freshly baked flat bread from the clay oven, humus, tahini, falafel and olives.

Around 9.30 Abdul Sharif stood up to deliver a speech of welcome to his honoured guests and to brief them on the plans for their 5-day visit. The next morning at 09.30 they were to be met by two Jeeps that would take them on a tour of the Step pyramid and the surrounding necropolis with him as the guide. They would return in time to freshen up again and be ready for a late lunch at about 14.00, where they were to enjoy a barbecued goat helped down with ice cold beer They were to be joined by his cousin, Zahi Awass director of antiquities and his wife. After lunch they were all to meet three surprise guests who had been waiting a very long time to meet them. He left that enigma floating in the air in spite of protestations from his guests. They all turned in to their comfortable lodgings for a night that was completely undisturbed from passing traffic, howls of hyenas, ghosts from the necropolis or by bowel infections caused by roto-viruses, bacteria such as salmonella or parasites such giardia.

The next morning, after a light breakfast of fresh fruit, yoghourt and black coffee, they set forth in two Jeeps driven by two of the staff. Leading the way, was the Jeep with Abdul Sharif up front and the Abrahams in the back seats. Following was the Sharif's chauffeur with Lucy and Angus in the back. They drove north west further into the desert for about 20 minutes and passed through the entry to the complex, bypassing the public parking lot, nodded through by the security staff, who had been alerted to this VIP visit. They eventually dismounted and the main crossing of the maze of cobbled paths. Facing them to the west was the giant step pyramid of

Djoser, looking north was the smooth and unimpressive pyramid of Teti and turning south west the third major pyramid of Sekhemkhet. Dotted all over the place were an abundance of mastaba, or over-ground tombs. The Pharaohs, Djoser and Sekhemkhet, were father and son and dated back in the mist of time, to the old kingdom of the third dynasty more than five thousand years in the past. Abdul Sharif then explained that the small Titi pyramid was perhaps the most important of them all, because they housed the "Pyramid Texts", the oldest religious writings in the world that made up the principal funerary literature of ancient Egypt. These texts were inscribed on the sarcophagi and walls within the pyramid in the 5th and 6th Dynasties of the Old Kingdom . The texts were reserved for the soul of the deceased pharaoh by his scribes and priests and were a series of spells and incantations designed to free the soul of the pharaoh from the body and help it ascend toward the heavens.

They were then led along a narrow causeway due west between the step pyramid and the Teti mound, towards a cluster of mastaba, with Lucy being invited to lead the way. She made straight for the last tomb on the west of the cluster and took over as the guide. Turning to the group and putting on a faux professorial tone of voice declaimed:

"Ladies and gentlemen let me introduce you to Ty, not tea, but T followed by Y.

I know Ty better than anyone in the world. I spent a year studying Ty, I gained my PhD thanks to Ty, and I earnt my chair of Egyptology thanks to Ty.

Ty lived under the reigns of several pharaohs, from the end of the 25th—the beginning of the 24th century BC. He was the husband of Princess Neferhetypes and was the Director of the hairdressers at the palace of the Pharaohs. Never patronise hairdressers, and in my next life, I wish to marry a hairdresser. In ancient Egyptian times, your hairstyle and your wigs announced your rank and wealth. Now follow me into his tomb and keep your heads down until I say." Bending low to slip through the hole in the rocks holding of the roof of the tomb, Lucy turned on her flashlight and invited the rest of the group to follow her. Once they were all inside, she shone her torch on the red granite sarcophagus, that was now empty with Ty's mummy being stored in the Cairo museum. She then slowly, with dramatic flourishes, moved the beam around the walls. They all burst out laughing at the pictures everywhere showing hairdressers at work with pictures of hairstyles and wigs exactly as you might find in a salon in Bond Street, Mayfair, London to this day.

After this delightful display they were free to wander around the park until 13.00 when they jumped back in the Jeeps to drive back to the Sharif's compound.

Just after 14.00, hungry and very thirsty, they gathered under the date trees outside the main villa, and sat down by a trellis table covered in a white cloth and bearing dozens of plates carrying Middle East delicacies, frothing pewter mugs of ice cold beer, and the burnt carcass of a roasted goat along the centre of the table. Servants carved great chucks of meat off the goat's flank and thighs. The English guests, who had never eaten goat before, were a bit timid at first, but with encouragement from the natives, soon tucked into what tasted like a cross between lamb and venison. About 30 minutes later a silver Mercedes E class limo arrived at the gates, and out stepped the very dapper figure of Abdul's cousin, the famous director of Egypt's department of antiquities accompanied by his glamorous wife, with bright lipstick, thick kohl eyeliner and elegant coiffure, just as if she had stepped out of the wall paintings of Ty's tomb. Introductions were made and hands were shaken around the table. The grandchildren were nowhere to be seen as they and their parents were having a siesta during the heat of the early afternoon. Once the midday feast was over, sweetmeats eaten and thimbles of Turkish coffee, sipped; there host stood up and made a little speech.

"Dear friends thank you for coming all this way to celebrate our golden wedding, it means a lot to us. 50 years may sound a long time to be married, but when you are in love like we are, the time flashes by." After a pause for applause and kisses from his wife, he continued. "In terms of the ancient Egyptians, whose homes we visited this morning, time has stood still. That then brings me to the point when I want to introduce you to our three special guests who have been housed in a guesthouse just outside the walls of the compound, so please follow me." Looking at each other in bewilderment, all the guest stood up and followed their host to the heat-controlled storage room housing the three mummies. On arrival, he threw open the double doors, turned on the lights, threw his hands in the air and cried out; "Voila, here are my unexpected guests, dug out of a hole in the ground nearby, where they have been passing the time for about 3,500 years!"

There was a deep inhaling of breath from the visitors accompanied by a squeal of horror from Sophie Abrahams. The first to respond amongst the baffled onlookers was Zahi Awass. "I know it's your Golden wedding Abdul and I understand you want to impress your visitors, but this is a breach of protocol and you know very well that you should have informed my department first." His cousin was not the least bit intimidated by the director of the department of antiquities and replied with a twinkle in his eye; " You are absolutely right dear Zahi, I'm a very naughty boy, but do not fear, I've completed the paperwork and made sure you would be amongst the first to see these finds." He then explained how he came across this trio of mummies and showed them the remains of the wooden sarcophagus before continuing; "Now before going any further let me know your immediate thoughts, starting with you dear cousin." There was no animus in this exchange as the two men had been best friends since boyhood and climbed their professional ladders in lockstep. Zahi Awass stood in silent musing, hand on chin, surveying the three corpses from a distance and having dismissed the two mummies with the clumsy linen wrap, stepped closer to the ceramic looking coffin and examined it carefully with a magnifying glass that appeared from a jacket pocket. After a few minutes in the hushed atmosphere of the workshop, he stood upright and passed an opinion. "Yes, Abdul you are a very naughty boy but then Zebras never change their stripes. These two mummies on the right are obviously workers from the Saqqara necropolis, the original occupants of the wooden sarcophagus, but this papier-mâché coffin is like nothing I've seen before. The outline looks like a female, and she must have been transferred to the sarcophagus at least 1,000 years after her two companions. I'm familiar with this kind of innermost coffins for the elite, and we have a few from the 18th dynasty Amarna period dated about 1,300 BCE, but I've never seen one so beautifully crafted as to look like ceramic with no obvious junction between the top and bottom halves. It must have been decorated all over with pictograms and cartouches, but these have faded away, but I can just make out an Ankh cross and the outline of a cartouche near the right foot. Here just by the right shoulder is the best clue I've found. It's the outline of a gazelle rearing on hind legs. That is a symbol of Amarna royalty. I'm sorry to disappoint you but this beauty will have to be transported to the laboratories at the Cairo museum as it's too precious for you to play about with. You are free to show your friends how to unwrap a mummy with her two companions."

As if on cue, Angus McCartney stepped forward and asked to borrow Dr Awass' magnifying glass, and turned to Abdul Sharif; "Do you have a torch and a large pair of scissors Professor? I want to have a closer look at the skin showing through the linen strips on this old fellow's abdomen." As the workshop was well stocked with the tools of the trade the two items were soon found and handed over and Abdul nodded his permission to make the first cut. With great care Angus slipped the sharp edge of the scissors under a strip of linen, gently folded the ends apart to protect the dry skin below which he examined with care through the magnifying glass under the light of the torch. After a moment or two he stood up to speak;

"Well, me lads and laddies, I'm a right knuckle-brained fart lozenge, if you'll forgive my French. This stuff showing through the gaps in the linen is not desiccated skin that looks like parchment, it's parchment that looks like desiccated skin. This old fellow has been wrapped in parchment with linen on top. What's more, the parchment has writing all over it. At a quick glance, it looks like it's been written in hieratic script from the period of the 18th dynasty of the new kingdom. I think these two old fellows must be companions of yon lassie and I guess it might tell us the story of how the three of them came to sleep together in that cedar box for the last 3,500 years. If so, this is the most important finding in my field since the discovery of the Edwin Smith and Ebers' papyruses in the 1860s. I support what Dr Awass said, all three of these mummies must be protected and moved to a facility where they can be studied by Xray and the wrapping of parchment removed by experts to be studied by a team led by me if I might be so bold." Abdul Sharif intervened from the chair he collapsed on in a state of shock. "Can we all come out of this workshop, lock it up safely, and join me for some iced tea and return to your seats at the table outside my villa. We need to plan very carefully how to proceed. This also the most important find of my career and I have been much longer in the game than Professor McCartney"

# CHAPTER 7

# MONDAY 6ᵀᴴ OF JANUARY 2020, THE DEPARTMENT OF ANATOMY, CAIRO MEDICAL SCHOOL

A FTER the anti-climax at Saqqara, the visitors settled down for a holiday at their host's generous invitation. The three mummies were shipped off, under tight security, to a safe room in the department of anatomy at the Cairo Medical school. Under normal circumstances, a find of this importance would have been researched in the great museum in Cairo under the supervision of Dr Awass, but much to his chagrin, the museum was in total disarray. The new, long-awaited Grand Egyptian Museum in Cairo, that should by now have been open for business, had been delayed by a year. That meant the second choice had to be in Abdul Sharif's bailiwick. The next decision to be made, was the membership of the team to carry out the work in the first few weeks of the new year. In order to save face, Professor Sharif voted that his cousin should head to the team and it made sense for Lucy and Angus to request leave of absence so they could add their expertise. There was a moment of discomfort when Zahi Awass begged Robert to join the team, with no one apart from his wife, aware that he had been suspended from his appointment pending investigations into the accusation of scientific misconduct. Awass himself was an expert in the genomics of the ancient Egyptians who had published a paper on Ancestry and pathology in King Tutankhamun's family 2010. As such he was well aware of Robert's expertise. After a moment's hesitation he chose the white lie that he would also seek leave of absence. Unfortunately, his wife could hardly choose "leave of absence" from her daughter whose new term at school started on January 3rd. In addition to those present they also had to recruit a team of experts in digital radiology and a specialist in the wrapping and burial of mummies in the new Kingdom 1500–1200 BCE. The last few days of holiday were spent sunbathing, jeep riding into the desert to visit nearby lesser known archaeological sites and best of all sophisticated chatter over ice cold alcoholic cocktails under the date palms during the happy hour.

Robert accompanied his wife to the airport at Cairo on the 29th of December to say fond farewells and promised her to be back home within three weeks.

On the first working day in the New Year, the team were gathered together in the small anatomical lecture theatre at the Cairo School of Medicine. Awass stood at the lectern and addressed the team of researchers who he labelled the Saqqara triplet team, SATT for short.

The newcomers were a French husband and wife duo, Cecile and Jean Baptiste DuToit, who were experts in the science of digital radiology of mummies, and Ingrid Johansen, born in Sweden but married to an Egyptian doctor, who had a PhD in the study of Ancient Egyptian mummification rituals. After introductions were complete and the team had pledged their confidentiality, he asked the lecture theatre technician to show the first slide. "Dear friends and colleagues we are about to embark on the study of a collection of three mummies discovered in the region of the Saqqara necropolis, the likes of which we haven't seen before. I will show the mummies together and then a series of closeups for a start and then ask you for your first impressions." His audience of seven, Professor Sharif, Robert Abrahams, Lucy Carpenter, Angus McCartney and the three newcomers, watched in silence until they came to the close ups of the lady in the ceramic coat, when Ingrid Johansen intervened. "This one is extraordinary, and I'll go as far as to say it's unique. This class of mummification is called cartonnage where the linen is covered with plaster mixed with crushed glass and polished to make a smooth surface. This covering of the cadaver was reserved for the elite and in all other examples I've seen, the smooth surface had been painted all over with the image of the face and hairstyle of the deceased that is lifelike, whilst the rest of the surface of the body and limbs is covered with pictograms of domestic or ceremonial scenes, pictures of the gods, often Osiris and Anubis, and a cartouche to give it an identity. I'll have to examine it more closely in a bright white light and ultra-violet, but from what I've seen already, it looks as if someone has taken great care to wipe the slate clean." Angus then addressed a question to Ingrid after asking for the close ups of the parchment showing through the linen wrap of the two male mummies. "Is there any precedent for parchment scrolls with written text to be included in the wrapping of a mummy?" "That's a good question Angus and one I've just been thinking about. It was commonplace for a papyrus scroll bearing the prayers from the 'Book of the Dead' to be found in a coffin but I've never seen such a scroll interleafed with the linen wrapping. Another mystery." They then discussed at length the agenda for the next few days. First, they would all visit the mummies in the secure laboratory to take their own pictures in different lighting whilst at the same time Cecile and Jean Baptiste carried out measurements for planning detailed radiological examinations of the mummies the next day. They would reconvene on Wednesday to review all the digital images and from thereon decide on the order of interventions to work through the layers and then study the physical remains of the bodies inside. Tuesday for the others would involve putting together the equipment and reagents for the biochemical analysis and carbon dating of the linen and parchments and for the analysis of any residual DNA that might have survived for nearly 3,500 years. Dr Awass and Robert Abrahams were hoping to find traces in bone marrow whilst Lucy would place her bets on hair follicles.

Apart from the two radiologists, wearing lead aprons, no one else was allowed in the secure room, much to the frustration of the rest of the crew but their discoveries were worth waiting for. 08.30 on Wednesday morning they reconvened to witness a well-rehearsed theatrical performance by Cecile and Jean Baptiste speaking in unison. "Mesdames et Messieurs, bien venue a notre son et lumière. Le premier acte, est la grande femme blanche—et VOILA- rien de tout!" The audience groaned as the outline of the white lady showed nothing other than a granular white image. Jean Baptiste then continued with a serious face, "Do not be sad, au contraire, this corpse has been wrapped in a radio-opaque material and has to be sheets of gold, which means, soit une Reine ou Princesse!" There were gasps and applause from the little audience. "We can offer you no more about this Royal lady until her cask has been cracked open and the gold plates have been removed. But for her two companions, we have much to show. I now hand over to my beautiful assistant, Cecile."

"Merci mon chère. I will show you all the images for the wrapped mummies side by side so that it will be easy to make comparisons. I will arrange the images in a way to display superficial first and then deeper layer by layer. For each anterior/posterior view, I have chosen a sagittal section at the level of the navel. The first set of images are focused at a depth of about 5 cm from the surface, the larger of the two was about 5ft 7ins in height and the other about 5ft 5ins, but to determine age and sex we will have to dig deeper. Of interest at this level on the sagittal slice, is that the larger corpse has layers of wrapping of different radiolucency, so that must be the one with the parchment showing through the linen. As we go deeper and deeper into the interior there is nothing of note except for the absence of metallic objects such as amulets or daggers. Now at this next level you get a beautiful image of the exterior of the cadavers, showing they are well preserved with no obvious evidence of trauma. Their heads are uncovered and probably shorn, and no obvious bracelets, rings or necklaces seen. Their shorn heads might suggest they were of the priestly caste. Wrapped in the linen of the larger man there are some strange looking artefacts that are not amulets and look more like the tools of his trade. Now of greatest interest is the next level where we can examine the skeleton in detail. Before we look at the bones please note that the abdominal cavity is stuffed with roles of linen, so far so normal. Looking at the pelvis, there is no doubt that both bodies are male and again no evidence of fractures either healed or post-mortem. Taking the smaller corpse first, his arms are held straight along his sides and from the dentition and epiphyseal junctions he would be between the age of 16 and 18. The fact that his dentition looks so healthy suggests he was one of the elite whose food was well cooked and free of grit. Looking at the larger figure, I would estimate he was in his mid-forties, he has lost some teeth but those that are preserved look healthy although the enamel looks worn. His left arm is flexed at the elbow with hand against his chest. His right arm hangs straight by his side and the hand is curled holding something metallic in its grasp. Now has anyone spotted what is unusual about these skeletons?" After a pause, Ingrid asked if they could see magnified views of the skull, following which, speaking slowly as if to control her excitement she announced: "The nasal and sphenoid bones in both skulls are intact, unlike all the other soft tissues, the brain has been left behind and I can see the desiccated brain tissue in the occipital region. This deviation from convention suggests to me that these two yummy mummies are from the Amarna period of the 18th dynasty!" Cecile clapped her hands slowly with typical French irony. "Mais oui mon petite fleur une vraie oeil de bœuf". Everyone laughed and the applause this time was sincere. Cecile and Jean Baptiste sat down and Professor Sharif step up to the lectern.

"Congratulations, a brilliant piece of detection and we are now off to a good start. If I could add one other suggestion, as neither of the bodies shows any sign of trauma, then apart from a case of poisoning, we have two healthy males aged between say 16 and 50 who have died of natural causes close in time. To me that suggests one the plagues that were endemic in that period. I think we should break for lunch and then reconvene to agree on the next steps."

After lunch they made a start on the young man now placed on a table at waist height. Ingrid was made responsible for opening up the linen wrap. She avoided the old-fashioned way of unwrapping the linen as if it were a toilet roll as that would entail rotating the mummy and risk the collapse of the fragile contents inside. Instead, using large scissors, she cut through the linen strips, one by one and layer by layer. There were only two very small amulets discovered, a tiny gold falcon and a larger scarab beautifully carved out of lapis lazuli.

She carefully preserved the scalp cover as the resin might have fixed some DNA from hair follicles. With all the linen flaps cut down the middle and opened like the pages of a book, there was a deep sigh from her little audience. Although the skin on the limbs and face were dark and desiccated, they were looking at a handsome youth with beautiful facial features stretched over a perfect skull and eyes closed as in slumber with long lashes intact. Nothing of interest was found in the abdominal or thoracic cavities, other than roles of linen. There was no evidence that this mummification process had been rushed and the amount of linen used suggested that the young man was a member of the elite.

Lucy now stepped forward to take her turn. She carefully ran her right hand over the bare cranium and under the occipital region but could find no evidence of surviving hair. She then gently plucked out a few eyelashes hoping there might be some DNA in surviving follicular material and placed them in sterile screw-top glass specimen bottles, and last of all cut some squares of the linen off the scalp and did the same.

Next Dr Awass and Robert Abrahams stepped forward with the tools of their trade. They gently drilled holes in the anterior surfaces of two lumbar vertebrae that were exposed and then turned their attention to the pelvic bones and scooped out any soft material with a sharp-edged spatula. Finally, they carefully chiselled through the nasal bones and the walls of the sinuses in the sphenoid bone. They then navigated this hole with a long-handled scoop and pushed until their tool hit the interior of the occipital bone and scraped out as much of the desiccated brain as they could find. It came out as granular tissue that was shared out in six sterile screw-capped bottles. Two were dry and the other four had different solutions for the fixing of biological material.

The time a flown and by now it was time to shut down the laboratory for the day and retire for drinks and dinner at Professor Sharif's townhouse. The cadaver of the young man was covered in a shroud out of respect and the material for DNA analysis was placed in the refrigerator to be transported to the molecular biology labs at the medical school the next day.

On Thursday morning they reassembled to examine the older man. The superficial layer of the linen wrap had obviously been done in a hurry allowing several gaps for the parchment to show through. It was now the turn of Angus to show his skills. Wearing a latex glove, with a torch and a magnifying glass in his hands, he surveyed the whole exposed surface of the parchment, carefully examining the edges where they turned down into the linen wrap below. With a pair of forceps, he tested the papyrus sheets for fixity to the under surfaces and stood up with a big smile. "This is going to be much easier than I thought. The parchment has been laid on the anterior surface of the mummy and has not been wrapped behind the back. It has not stuck down suggesting all the resin in the linen below had dried out and I guess that it was added several months after the initial mummification." They had prepared a long marble table to receive the parchments with a plate of glass of matching size. There were four pages of very high-quality papyrus carrying the written words that in some places the black ink had been interrupted with lines of script coloured in red. The pages each measured 50 x 50 cm, were then slid onto a slate tile covered in talc and then placed in order from top-down, onto the marble-topped table. Angus then matched them up close side by side and saw a perfect fit and what he guessed would be the right order, following which, he and Lucy gently laid down the glass top over the realigned the 200 cm scroll.

Below the stratum of the parchment, they could now see a perfectly embalmed body.

Ingrid of the long scissors cut her way through copious layers of best quality linen meeting some surprising artefacts along the way. There were some beautiful amulets of conventional design but also what looked like paintbrushes and pallets made out of red agate and lapis.

When they got down to the cadaver, there was an obvious likeness to the youth he accompanied to the afterlife. In his right hand he held a bronze adze and in his left hand held up to his chest, he clutched a gold disc bearing the sun symbol of the Aten.

Specimens for the genomics were harvested in the same way as for the youth who was in all likelihood, his son.

By then it was time to finish for the day and Dr Awass and Professor Sharif had important meetings the following day, and as they had made such great progress, they decided to start work on the genomics of the samples and the translation of the Saqqara codex on Monday the 13th December. Cecile and Jean Baptiste for dismissed for the time being but would be recalled when they next met to discuss the results of their findings.

For the next two weeks both teams, genome and script, worked feverishly with the help of several technicians who had no idea what the excitement was all about.

It soon became clear that Robert could not keep his promise to his wife that he would be home in three weeks. By the time the two teams met up again, it was January 30th.

They all agreed that their results were astonishing and paved the way for cracking open the white capsule holding the corpse of a mysterious member of a Royal Household.

As they were congratulating each other the mobile phones of the three English professors went off almost synchronously. Each caller was a staff member of the British embassy in Cairo who advised them to return home immediately as the WHO had just declared a global pandemic of a dangerous new virus known as COVID-19. They were warned that it was only a matter of time for all air travel to be closed down. Shortly after that Robert got a call from Sophie in London, begging him to come home on the next available flight.

Almost in tears, the group split up hugging each other in a farewell embrace and promising to meet again once the plague had passed over. The lady in the white carapace would have to await their return.

# CHAPTER 8

# NAUCRATIS, JANUARY 30TH, 2020

FOLLOWING the tsunami, there were many evil omens, portents, miracles and wonders.

A docked barge in southern Egypt leaked almost 100 tons of gasoline into the Nile River after the tidal wave caused it to tilt and partially submerge, allowing the fuel to leak out.

The vessel was docking in Aswan, a city about 700 miles south of Cairo when part of it sank beneath the surface and began to spew red crude oil into the river. Officials in Luxor downriver from Aswan, announced states of emergency after the spill reached their water purification station. The crude oil looked the colour of blood. The river then became full of dead fish. These were the fish that thrive on frog spawn. As a result, two months later, there was an epidemic of frogs. That year's locust season had been the worst in a generation. Hundreds of billions of insects, in thick and devastating swarms, had descended on crops in a corridor of destruction from the north of Sudan and devastated the crops as far north as Qena. All that was needed to complete the Biblical narrative of Exodus, was the plague.

On January the 30th, about four months after his accident, David Goddard also received a phone call from the British embassy, advising him to fly back to the UK as soon as possible.

His response is worth recording. "Not a bloody plague as well! I appreciate your concern about my welfare, but I'm perfectly happy where I am so piss off and leave me alone!"

To say he was perfectly happy was an understatement, he had never been so happy in his life he had found Nirvana. He was in love, he had an adopted son, he loved the villagers who had been so hospitable and best of all his leg was healed and he was now free to explore the depths of the river Nile just outside his front door. How all this came to pass needs to be recounted.

On his return from the visit to the General hospital at Abu Hummus, David was in a state of deep depression. Hobbling along on crutches, in a little village at the back of beyond, no one spoke good English and all his possessions were lost. No one to miss him at home and his closest friends and colleagues were dead. No alcohol to drown his sorrow and no woman to offer comfort. Over the next few days, he even contemplated suicide. The villagers couldn't have been more hospitable and kinder. They fitted out his temporary shelter in the archaeological ruins nearby with mats made from the bulrushes, a simple wooden bed with a straw-filled mattress, an old chair and a bedside table painted to look like something from the days of the Pharaohs. On the table, they mounted an oil lamp and threw over the bed a simple colourful patchwork quilt. They fashioned a temporary toilet in a walled-off corner of the ruins and invited him to use the shower in the backyard of the family who first offered him succour.

The boy from the household Ahmed, whose full name was Ahmed Hussein ibn Mustafa, spent an hour with him each day after school to improve his English and in return teach him rudimentary conversational Arabic. His mother, in the raiment of mourning, brought him breakfast and an evening meal. She never spoke and always held her head down almost looking like a hunchback. He got to enjoy his new middle eastern diet, with freshly baked flatbread, hummus, tahini, falafel, olives, fresh fruit and vegetables along with cups of black bittersweet coffee. Once a week on a Friday evening they would enjoy lamb shaslik or lamb kebab. Most evenings the elders of the village accompanied by Ahmed joined him, to enjoy a smoke, some coffee and the telling of tales whilst sitting around a fire pit, with Ahmed acting as interpreter. Life settled into a quiet and predictable routine, but he still had little hope for his future.

All this changed in the early morning of the 21st of October, three weeks after his arrival. It had been a hot and humid night and he couldn't sleep so at midnight he decided to take a cold shower in the ibn Mustafa back yard. As he struggled to find his way in the moonlit landscape, he was sure he heard the sound of splashing water. Looking around the corner he was stunned to see the back view of a naked woman standing tall in the shower stall, with her head tilted upwards into the torrent of water, and long luxurious hair reflecting gold in the midnight. Her posture and long sinuous body were erotic and aesthetic and the same time, very much like his first glance at his favourite model in the life classes of his London studio. Feeling somewhat ashamed, he stepped behind the trunk of a date palm, a gave a little cough.

The lovely lady did not scream but kept her self-control, held a towel up to cover her nakedness and quietly asked, "Min hunak?" which David translated as "who is there?"

He replied "'Iinah 'ana", it is I. At that, the lovely lady in the moonlight burst out laughing and to his amazement responded in English. "Mr Goddard, I guessed it was you, but your pronunciation is terrible." "Who are you, and how do you know my name?" replied David.

Adopting a coquettish tone, she replied, "So you don't recognise me, Sir, I serve you breakfast every morning, I am Ahmed's mother, and my name is Aisha."

In retrospect, he always said it was love at first sight but at the time he was more curious than aroused. "How come you speak such good English?" "Well Mr Englishman, if you would allow me to dry myself and put on clothes, I will bring you some coffee to your little house and then we can sit in the beautiful moonlight and I can tell you my tale."

David hobbled back to his hovel leaning against the surviving walls of the walls of ancient Naucratis. To say there was a spring in his step is perhaps a misnomer, but had it not been for his crutches and his fractured ankle, he might have danced the cha-cha. He quickly dragged out his chair and placed it near the base of a 4,000-year-old marble pillar, that he used when sitting out of doors, that happened to be directly illuminated by a full moon and waited patiently.

20 minutes later, Aisha glided into the moonlight carrying a brass tray bearing a bronze copper *dallah* pot with a long spout looking like the beak of an Ibis. Her hair was wrapped in a turban and she wore a colourful flowing kaftan that hid her feet. She placed the tray on the ground and served the dark fragrant coffee into two porcelain *cawa* cups bearing Arabic calligraphy. Seeing her face in full light for the first time, his heart missed a beat as he thought he recognised her, but it took a while to realise whom

she resembled. They both had a sip of the sweetened coffee flavoured with cardamom before she spoke:

"David, if I may? My story is a bit of a cliché if you'll forgive me. It's the same old story of a rich spoilt princess falling in love with a poor but handsome fisherman. You may think that modern Egypt is a classless society unlike the strict class system of our ancient ancestors. They had five castes we have only three. About 10 per cent of Egypt's population are obscenely rich and can afford to live in the gated communities in houses that cost millions of dollars. The 40 per cent in the middle-class struggle to afford a humble desert home, whilst the 50 per cent who make up the poorest stratum of our population can't even dream about owning or renting a home. In the cities, they live in ramshackle slums or even amongst the headstones of Cairo's necropolis, whilst in the country they can at least preserve their dignity by building huts made of any material at hand. You will have noticed that our village has been built with mud bricks we fashioned ourselves with roofs made of reeds or corrugated iron. We can even improve on these modest materials by illegally helping ourselves to some of the granite and marble stone from the archaeological site next door. Our elders pay a little protection money so the inspectors will turn a blind eye. You then have to appreciate the fact that the elite in our society wishes to retain or enhance their ranking in society by placing a premium on marital and family stability. They see marriage as a decision not just for individuals, but for parents and the extended family. So, in practice, most marriages are still arranged to some extent and are determined by the level of the income of a potential spouse."

By this time David's jaw figuratively dropped on listening to her educated voice and command of English. His inner voice spoke in words not fit to be said in front of a lady like this, "Bugger me, she speaks better English than what I do!". She paused to take a sip of coffee allowing David to translate his inner voice into socially acceptable words.

"Aisha, If I may? Your English is perfect and probably better than mine. You must have been very well educated to master our tongue to build up such a good vocabulary."

"And that Mr Englishman was part of the problem. My parents spent a fortune on my education, I went to the best schools in Cairo, spent a year at a finishing school in Dorset, and then entered the University of Alexandria to study the classics. In my second year, during the winter vacation, together with six of my girlfriends, we hired a dhow to sail down to Saqqara to visit the step pyramid and its surroundings. We spent three nights sleeping onboard and that is when I fell in love with Mustafa. He was very handsome, well-built and with a lovely smile, but by then I'd been courted by many such men. The difference with Mustafa was his kind eyes that sparkled with humour and intelligence. He was a very poor man from a very poor family who had been denied an education. I took it upon myself to make up for this deficiency on the second night of our voyage and then as you English say with your gift for understatement, 'one thing led to another'" Aisha paused for another sip of coffee but couldn't disguise the moistness of her eyes. David was about to interrupt when she put a finger to her lips. "Needless to say, my parents, brothers, aunts and uncles, were furious and when I became pregnant with Ahmed who is now 16, they couldn't bear the shame. I was disinherited and kicked out of the house and I've never seen my family since that day. Mustafa and I married before our son was born and his family embraced me. They and the other villagers are the kindest and most hospitable people on this planet. The only problem was that they were very traditional in their ways and I had some difficulty bending my will to their beliefs and traditions. My secularism and scholarship were an embarrassment to them as much as they were mandatory in my parent's house. In the end, I adapted to this new lifestyle, but I do miss the opportunities for enjoying a conversation like this. It was my greatest ambition to give our son the opportunity of going to a good school and then on to University and Mustafa and I were saving up for that purpose. To boost his income of his daytime job as a fisherman, he also moonlighted running cruises up and down the Nile for tourists to witness the Sphinx and the pyramids at Giza literally by moonlight. A year ago, he was gunned down by terrorists searching for westerners under the blank gaze of the sphinx.

I accepted my role as a widow in mourning according to custom until yesterday. As chance would have it, you caught me in the shower obeying ritualistic custom for purifying the spirit after a year of mourning. You are the first to see me with my hair down and now wearing coloured apparel in 12 months." She then turned her head as the tears ran down her cheeks.

David, with some difficulty, restrained his instinctive reaction to put his arm around her by way of comfort.

After about five minutes of silent introspection, Aisha turned around and looked at David with the cool gaze of the woman he had secretly loved for the last 35 years. He had met her for the first time at the Uffizi Gallery in Florence, her name was Lucrezia, and she was 450 years old but didn't look a day older than 35. She was the wife of the Venetian ambassador to Florence and was painted by Angelo Bronzino. As far as David was concerned, she was a living, breathing quintessence of womanhood. She wears an opulent necklace that states on several small beads that love last eternally - *Amour Dure Sans Fin*—clearly alluding to love and faithfulness. On her left ring finger, she carries a gilded ring with a nestled dark emerald stone, a synonym of engagement in Western society. Yet her beauty outshines her sumptuous raiment and priceless jewellery.

She was more than conventionally beautiful with pouting lips and green-grey luminous eyes but was mysterious and unattainable and gazed at the onlooker with interest as if there was a question on her lips. Her intelligence was not only in her eyes but in the confident way she held her head high on her curvaceous neck. Her skin was faultless, and the shape of her face was enhanced by a high forehead and a hairstyle of a tight plat wound around her crown. The open book on her right knee held in place by her bejewelled right hand, was the artist's iconography to acknowledge her scholarship. David never forgot their first face to face meeting and could always summon her up in his dreams. Since then he made several visits to Florence, going straight to the octagonal room where she was always waiting to see him and to hold him hypnotised in her cool gaze. And now he found her in the flesh sitting in the moonlight under the arch of an ancient Egyptian temple in the back of the beyond.

His first thought was, "Now I've found her I will never let her go."

From that midnight tryst onwards they both subconsciously knew where things would lead. Their courting was decorous and covertly had won the approval of Aisha's in-laws and the delight of young Ahmed. When it was time for David to have the cast removed from his leg, it seemed perfectly natural for Aisha to accompany him. Once Dr Yacoub pronounced that all was well and he could now be discharged and fly back home, his immediate response came as a surprise to both doctor and lady friend. "Am I now fit to swim in the Nile?". He then began to reiterate his story of how he ended up amongst the bulrushes at Naucratis, but then went on to disclose the secret of the ancient Egyptian chariot buried in the sands of time. Dr Yacoub was intrigued but had no reason to deny him the right to swim but was sceptical of his chances of seeing this chariot again.

The next day he collected his sub aqua kit minus the empty air tanks and followed by Ahmed, Aisha and half the village, walked to the riverbank where his buoy was still bobbing up and down to mark the spot where he had surfaced three months ago. He put on his wet suit, facemask and snorkel, intending to dive down to see if there were still any signs of the underwater treasure. Ahmed had insisted on joining him as he was a skilled swimmer and could hold his breath underwater for nearly three minutes. They both slipped into the river and dived down vertically to the area beneath the buoy. David resurfaced first having seen nothing but sand and was alarmed that Ahmed remained underwater for further 60 seconds. He re-emerged with a big smile on his face and a throwing stick in his hand to the astonishment of his mentor. David examined it carefully, knowing that modern versions of throwing sticks were used to this day in hunting waterfowl, but Ahmed insisted that it was ancient because he found it trapped between the spokes of a wheel that peaked through the riverbed. On closer examination they were just able to make out the etchings of hieroglyphics, but it was beyond the skills of Goddard to give it a precise date. He then asked Ahmed to join him again in a dive and to try and guide him to the spot. Yes, he had not fantasised his find, sure enough a chariot wheel bonded with gold could just be seen at the surface of the detritus at the bottom of the Nile. He swam back to retrieve his buoy and dived back down to attach its lanyard to a spoke in the wheel.

That day his happiness was complete, sitting by the remains of the fire in the pit by his hut, he picked out some charcoal a drew a beautiful portrait, on a scrap of paper amongst the discarded wrappings, of Aisha who was sitting by his side. "Dearest Aisha, with this sketch I pledge my everlasting love. Will you marry me and let me act as a loving stepfather to your son. If you say yes, I will promise to find the money to send Ahmed to the best school in this district and from there to University." Aisha found this an offer she couldn't refuse and that night there were celebrations all round, a goat was roasted, and the headman of the village happened to find an odd bottle of Dimple Haig to toast the happy couple. The manner of a wedding between an atheistic Christian and a secular Muslim was of no consequence because the villages covertly worshiped the pagan gods of ancient times and were sure that Hathor goddess of love and fertility would approve.

CHAPTER 9

# THE PLAGUE AND ITS AFTERMATH

T HE term "butterfly effect" was coined by meteorologist Edward
Lorenz, who discovered in the 1960s that tiny, butterfly—scale
changes to the starting point of his computer weather models, re-
sulted in anything from sunny skies to violent storms at distant parts of the
globe, with no way to predict in advance what the outcome might be. And
with that observation, he laid down the foundation of chaos theory.

In these days of lazy thinking, this picturesque concept has been replaced by the meme, "actions have consequences". Indeed, they do.

A man in China eats a bat burger from a stall in the wet market of
Wuhan and the world is in lockdown from the worst viral pandemic in
living memory.

The economy goes into the worst global recession since the 1920s, and
unemployment is at a record height.

A policeman's knee throttling a black man in Minneapolis, and we
have the worst race riots in living history. Statues of prominent slave traders are pulled down and Winston Churchill's statue in parliament square
is defaced. These riots and countered by the neo Nazi groups and gangs
of football thugs, intent on "protecting" Churchill's statue who attack the
police giving Hitler salutes and chanting "we are racists and we don't care."
The anti-Zionists can't miss a chance like this and the "free Palestine" flag
can be seen outside the besieged American embassy. In Paris, they go one
step further and chant "dirty Jews, dirty Jews". So, it's not a surprise to see
who gets the blame on Twitter for spreading the virus and teaching the

American police the tactics of brutality, Israel of course. Then on cue, the anti-vaccination lobby joins in with their set of grievances.

The scene was set for a perfect storm on June 13th, the Queen's official birthday. This occasion was not marked by the traditional trooping of the colour but a private event within the walls of Windsor Castle, where a shrunk down band of the first battalion Welsh Guards, marched up and down in front of her majesty, maintaining the two-metre social distancing, whilst banging their drums and blowing their trumpets.

This sad scene was being watched by Robert Abrahams with his wife and daughter who had been hunkering down in their North West London home for more than three months when his mobile phone beeped to remind him of the Zoom meeting he was to attend with his friends and colleagues from the Saqqara Triplet Team. Much had happened in his life in spite of the lockdown. He had been completely exonerated of the accusations of scientific misconduct after investigations suggested that his computer had been accessed by a stranger. It was not too difficult for a forensic team to pick up fingerprints other than those the departmental head and as soon as all those with access to Robert's office were invited to be tested his chief technician confessed. To avoid a scandal the culprit was invited to take early retirement and allowed to keep his pension fund providing he would tell the police who was behind the plot. Needless to say, the offenders had already left the country and were now living somewhere in Jerusalem.

The work on the ancient DNA from the Saqqara mummies was almost ready for publication with two teams collaborating. In Cairo, the lockdown had been much looser than in London, but Robert and one other technician were allowed access to their labs that doubled up as part of a forensic team helping the Metropolitan Police. He couldn't wait to tell his friends about their latest findings.

At 15.00 BST in the UK and 16.00 in Egypt, the Saqqara eight appeared in their windows on Zoom. A new technology that by happenstance served the needs of the global lockdown.

Dr Awass took the chair and the updated reports were delivered at his command. Prof Sharif went first almost bursting with excitement. As his builders continued working on what was to become the sewerage tank for the extension of his villa, they found themselves blocked by ancient underground walls. These turned out to be the remains of an ancient burial chamber that had been appropriated for the burial of the three mummies. So, they had not been buried without ceremony in a dugout pit, they had simply taken over the resting place of one of the architects of the stepped pyramid as judged by the wall paintings.

Ingrid had little to offer other than the carbon dating of the linen wraps that showed that the outer and inner layers of the large man were of the same epoch. She also confirmed that he must have an artist and sculptor, who worshiped the Aten as judged by the sun disk held over his heart.

Lucy also had little new to add but was complimented for her involvement in the Black Lives Matter campaign. She was frequently on the TV, a voice a reason who called out those parasites who were trying to hijack their cause for their own hidden agenda.

Angus had finished his work on the carbon dating and complete translation of the papyrus role.

Robert Abrahams had something new and exciting to report as well. His technical assistant was working on a doctorate thesis in paleo-virology. Since the late 1980s "viral fossils" had been detected in ancient skeletons and mummies. In the 1990s, double primer polymerase chain reactions (PCR) had made the job of identifying long lost viral RNA of retroviral material embedded in the DNA of a host cell, possible. Most recently the use of high-throughput Next Generation Sequencing (NGS) techniques in the field of ancient DNA research had facilitated reconstruction of the genomes of ancient or extinct organisms. He has been able to identify the fingerprint of a coronavirus in the brain material of the large man that confirms his death from a plague but what was even more remarkable, this viral fossil looks like a close relative to COVID-19.

Everyone started talking at the same time until Dr Awass called the group to order.

"What you've just described, Professor Abrahams, strengthens my decision on how to proceed. We can no longer delay publication until it is again safe for us to reconvene to study the woman in white, there is pressure on me to disclose our findings so far, there were too many witnesses to our work and the gossip has already provoked telephone calls from newspapers journalists and TV producers. Even if there is an infinitesimal chance of your findings leading to a vaccine that might exploit cross-immunity we must make our findings public. I suggest that Professor Sharif is the first author of the paper of the findings in his back yard, you Angus lead on the translation of the codex and you David lead on the molecular genealogy." The only dissent from this plan was from Abdul Sharif he suggested he was last author whereas Ingrid, with a great future ahead of her went first.

They then discussed at length the journals they would choose.

They agreed on the Journal of Egyptian Archaeology for the first two papers and Nature for the third.

CHAPTER *10*

# THE SAQQARA CODEX

Translation and Interpretation, of a narrative papyrus discovered in the wrappings of a mummy from Amarna period discovered in the necropolis at Saqqara. McCartney A. et al, The Journal of Egyptian Archaeology, Vol. 122, pp 35-52, September 1st, 2020.

## Introduction

The circumstances and the detailed positioning of three mummies from the 18th dynasty Amarna period have already been described in the paper by Johansen I. et al, in this edition of the J. Egyptian Archaeology.[1] One of these mummies carried the corpse a middle-aged man who seemed to have died of natural causes. By the artefacts included in the mummification process, it was determined that in life he served a royal household as an artist and a sculptor. The most unusual finding in the investigation of the mummy was a very well-preserved papyrus scroll that had been cut up into squares and wrapped in its superficial linen strips. The excellent condition of the papyrus can be accounted for by its protective cover of resin and the very dry atmosphere in a cedar wood sarcophagus buried two metres below the surface of the desert plain. Carbon dating of the papyrus and

1. Johansen I et al; Three new mummies from the Amarna Period discovered at Saqqara. The Journal of Egyptian Archaeology, Vol. 122, pp 27–34, September 1st, 2020.

the ink confirmed that it was produced in the period 1,300–1,2000 BC. An original scroll of 200cm had been neatly cut into 4 squares 50 x 50cms. They were realigned on a table side by side in a way that made sense of the sequence. The writing was in hieratic script by a very skilled scribe, the ink was black with one section emphasised in red ink. All the technical details for handling the material are described in the annex.

# The translation

I address this to the perfect God the only one whose beauty the Orb created and the will of him who begot him who satisfies him would what pleases his spirit who does effective things for him who begot him who controls the land for him.

My father the living advocate of the Aten of the two horizons who rejoices on the horizon in his name of light which is the essence of the orb give life forever and my heart is joyful because of the King's wife and her children. Granting a great age to the King's great wife Neferneferuaten who lives forever and ever in these millions of years and granting a great age to the King's daughters Meritaten and the King's daughter Meketaten and her children under the authority of the King wife their mother forever or ever, this is my true oath which is my will to declare and I will not abjure forever and ever.

How manifold are your deeds though hidden from sight, sole God apart from whom there is no other! You created the earth according to your desire when you were alone, people cattle and flocks all upon earth that walk on legs or on the high that fly with wings, the foreign lands of the Levant and Kush the land of Egypt, you put everyman in his place you supply their needs everyone has his food and his allotted life span their tongues differ in speech their characters likewise, their skins are different because you made the foreigners distinct, you created the inundation in the underworld and you bring it forth as you desire you let the common people live just as you made them for yourself. Their Lord of war who wearies himself for them. The Lord of every land who rises for them, the Orb the of the daytime great in majesty. All far off lands you make them live. You have placed an inundation in the sky that it might descend for them and create waves upon the mountain, like the sea, to irrigate their fields in their locality how effective are your plans O Lord of eternity.

Now listen to my demands so that when you enter the afterlife you can bow to the Orb and say with a true heart:

*I have not done people wrong*

*I have not done wrong in the place of truth*

*I have done no evil*

*I have not caused my name to become tainted as a slave master*

*I have not deprived a poor man of his property*

*I have not caused pain*

*I have not created hunger*

*I have not killed*

*I have not given orders to kill*

*I have not fornicated*

*I have not committed fraud*

*I have not taken milk from the mouths of children*

*I have not extinguished the flame*

*I will not worship other gods or their effigies even though they may be images of the mother that you loved, may she rest in peace for eternity*

My name is Tuthmose, and I am the high priest of the Aten. Here you will find the mummified remains of the three most beloved members of my family. My royal mother, my venerated father, and the young brother Amenhotep, all of whom died of the plague. My father Thutmose was the great artist to the royal household and made exquisite figurines of my Royal mother, Neferneferu-aten, who gave birth to me in bull rushes to keep her secret and presented me as crown prince to the assembly in the second year of her regency after the death of her husband, Akhenaten the first to declare the Aten, the one and only God.

May young breath, the sweet breeze of the north wind, go forth into the sky on the arms of the living, protected in their hearts content, no evil can affect their limbs, they will remain whole and their bodies will never putrefy as they follow the Orb as he rises at day break . Come for their souls wherever it is, come for their souls o guardians of the heavens, may their souls live on in their mummified bodies which will never be destroyed or perish.

They were buried at the Royal burial ground on the east bank of the Nile where the sun rises and not like the followers of heathen Gods on the West Bank of the great river where the Orb always sets.

Our passage from mastery of the known world, the great empire of Egypt, under the guidance and blessing of the Aten, is a sorry story of loss, bereavement and suffering.

Our blessed mother, co Regent of the kingdom, who shared the throne with our godfather the great Pharaoh Akhenaten, for many years, became the only Pharaoh after his death in the 15th year of his reign. She died in great pain from the curse of the cold bulging tumour of the breast, two years ago and was buried with full honours in the necropolis alongside the side of the great Temple of the Aten, in a magnificent shrine, with her earthly remains protected in six coffins and bound in gold. After her death the boy Tutankhamen, the only son of Akhenaten, whose mother was the whore whose name will not be spoken, became King. He had no wisdom of his own and regents from the sects of Amun-Ra, Osiris, Horus, Thoth and Hathor, denounced the followers of the one and only God, the Aten. They sent their men at arms to deface our temple and destroy the images of Aten. It was I, at the age of 16 had my hair shorn and was anointed a priest to serve the forbidden God. My father, Tuthmose, at that time, following the death of Akhenaten, had been anointed high priest by my mother. He decreed that effigies of Gods were not to be worshiped; he a common sculptor could make many images of gods, but the one true God cannot be looked at in the face lest you become blinded. Following the destruction of our temple, we who were living in Amarna were subject to heavy taxes and forbidden to worship the Orb on pain of death. Many of our young men were drafted into the armies of the new king and many of our daughters were taken into slavery. We could not protect them as we were not allowed to bear arms on pain of death. Then swarms of locusts from the dark lands of Nubia, destroyed all our crops and famine led to the deaths of many of our little ones. Plague struck us again and I lost my father and my young brother Amenhotep, who were buried in humble coffins alongside the shrine of my noble mother as all our gold and precious woods and stones had been taken as taxes by the army of the boy king. Finally, the regents of the upper and lower land of Egypt decreed that all those who worshiped the Aten, must renounce their faith and return to the worship of the old gods lest they die. Their messengers alerted us that the armies of Tutankhamen from Memphis in the north and Thebes in the south would arrive the next day.

I spoke unto my people and offered them a choice to either obey the edict of the king and stay or join me to flee from this place to find a place of safety in the desert west of the Nile.

All agreed to follow my leadership and begged me to bring along the mummies of my mother, father and brother to be at the centre of a shrine when we find a place of safety.

I then ordered all the women to make flat bread to take on our journey, enough food for 10 days, we had 9 camels to carry water, and a cart with two oxen to carry the three mummies, for I had determined to rest by the pyramid of Saqqara, where I was aware of many hiding places. All the men then gathered by the blocked entrance to the burying chambers of my family. The strongest amongst us broke down the wall. The mummies of my father and brother were easy to carry out from their simple wooden coffins. My mother's shrine took many hours to break into and we only had the strength to carry her innermost coffin. Because it was covered in beautiful colours and images with a perfect likeness of her face that had been painted by my grieving father, I gave the order to wash off all the paint so that it would never be an idol of worship before she was carried out of the catacombs to lead us on our way into the desert where the Aten sets at night. The night before the arrival of the detachments of the king's army arrived, our small procession of 40 men, their families and 100 of our loyal servants, crossed the river to the west and turned north to follow the river in the direction of Saqqara. Some of our servants who had come from Nubia where sent east up into the mountainous zone that had formed a protective bowel for our beloved royal city of Amarna, carrying flares and beacons to provide a decoy when the soldiers of the king arrived. They were well rewarded and hoped to escape to the south in a hazardous journey back to the land of their birth.

I write these words with a heavy heart. We reached the necropolis at Saqqara after walking for nearly 10 days. Although the women and children took turns on riding the camels, the beasts themselves were exhausted and our supplies of bread, water and wine depleted. The local villages knew nothing of a plight and assumed we were either nomads or traders who often past along this route. They were happy to supply us with enough food and water to continue our journey to the flat lands, east of the Nile delta. We had no idea how long it would take for the king's soldiers to catch up with us, but we found that carrying the three mummies was burdensome, as it set the pace of the two bullocks dragging the two wheeled cart, on which they lay. Whilst everyone rested that first night, together with my two most loyal servants, I made a reconnoitre of the periphery necropolis to see if I could find an empty mastaba that we might requisition as a resting place for our three sacred cadavers. We found one quite easily at the south eastern edge of the sanctified ground where only the humblest of the artisans were buried. The following morning, we transferred the three mummies to this safe place, sealed the doorway and painted some images of scribes and farmers together with simple cartouches that fit their lowly status.

My plan was to find a way across the reed-sea of the delta and turn northward to the land of the Canaanites and the tribes who lived east of the Jordan river. Although part of the Egyptian empire they had many grievances and I planned to convert them to our ways and raise an army to conquer the lower kingdom. I could then retrieve the earthly remains of my beloved family and rebury them in a great Temple I will build in honour to the one God, the Orb, the Aten.

But first, we must find a way of crossing to the other side of the great river, nay the Red sea, that has sustained the lives of generation after generation to the beginning of time thanks to the will and blessing of our Lord, the Aten.

# Discussion

The four sections of the papyrus scroll appear to have come from two separate sources. The first is clearly a declaration of the creed of the worshippers of the Aten written in formal language, whilst the second is a narrative that explains how the parchments ended up underground close to the Saqqara necropolis. As far as the first section is concerned, the text highlighted in red might appear to be an adumbration of the Biblical 10 commandments. This is not the first time they've been witnessed and something very like this was discovered on a papyrus unearthed by Flinders Petrie, during his early excavations of Amarna in 1891.[2]

There is also some resonance here to the *Al Chait* prayers that are chanted by Jewish worshipers on Yom Kippur, the day of atonement.

The second half of the manuscript is of much greater importance to Egyptologists as it resolves many uncertainties about the Amarna period.

Most of the mummies from the period in question come from the two great Royal caches found in the late 19th century ( TT32O and KV-35 the

---

2. File Petrie MSS 1.11 - *Petrie Journal* 1891 to 1892 (Amarna) Oxford University.

tomb of Amenhotep II in the Valley of the Kings) which revealed most, but not all of the Kings reigning between the 17th and 20th dynasties. Among the "missing" Kings (as identified at the beginning of the 20th century) were Akhenaten and Tutankhamun. A few Queens were found in KV-320 but none later than Ahmes-Nefertiry the wife of Ahmose I. Thus, the bodies of Akhenaten and Nefertiti became part of a "wanted" list of ancient royalty. For many the search Akhenaten came to an end in 1907 when tomb KV-55 was found in the Valley of the Kings, this deposit amongst other things contained funerary shrine of Queen Tiye the wife of Amenhotep III and mother of Akhenaten and along with this were artefacts bearing the name of Akhenaten and a gilded glass inlaid wooden coffin from which all names and the face mask have been removed. This is how a heretics mummy might have been defaced and in the 1960s the speculation was supported by comparing blood groups with that of the corpse of Tutankhamen. Final confirmation followed DNA testing in the 1990s. Furthermore, the published interpretation of the DNA data the "younger lady" (the 'whore' described in the scroll) showed her as a full sister of Tutankhamen's father and there is absolutely no indication that Nefertiti was the sister wife of her husband, indeed, the fact, that on no occasion does she use the titles King's daughter or King's sister, makes it all but certain that she was not.[3] So to this day the whereabouts of the mummy of Neferneferuaten (Nefertiti) has remained unknown. There can be little doubt that the "ceramic" coffin contains the mummy of this legendary queen. Her coffin and its contents will be studied by the team who found her once foreign travel is resumed. Sadly, her death in pain from a "cold bulging tumour of the breast" almost certainly refers to breast cancer as described in the medical text, "The Edwin Smith" papyrus.[4] There is much in both sections of the parchment, that reinforces the concept that Akhenaten was the founder or restorer of monotheism, as first suggested by Sigmund Freud.[5]

Apart from the discovery of Nefertiti's remains, the other finding of great interest, is the suggestion that Tuthmose the Royal artist, had a love

3. C. Aldred. *Akhenaten, King of Egypt: a new study*. London: Thames & Hudson, 1968, 153–62; A. Dodson. *Amarna Sunrise: Egypt from Golden Age to Age of Heresy*. Cairo: American University in Cairo Press, 2014, 163–65

4. Breasted, James Henry. *The Edwin Smith Surgical Papyrus: published in facsimile and hieroglyphic transliteration with translation and commentary in two volumes*. University of Chicago Oriental Institute Publications, v. 3–4. Chicago: University of Chicago Press, 1991. First published 1930.

5. Freud, Sigmund (1939). Moses and Monotheism. Hogarth Press, 1939.

child with Nefertiti ("found in the bulrushes"!), who fathered the writer of the Saqqara codex. Tuthmose was as famous in his lifetime as he is to this day having created the iconic bust of Nefertiti in all her glory, that found its way to the Berlin Museum.[6] Less well known is that his studio at Amarna, excavated by Flinders Petrie in the late 19th C, contained many works that celebrated her beauty that included full length curvaceous statues, with her body wrapped in tight see-through pleated linen. He clearly was obsessed with her and would not have been the first artist to fall in love and have a child with his favourite model!

The narrative of their flight from Amarna to Saqqara bearing the bodies of Nefertiti, Thutmose and their second son, Amenhotep, perfectly describes the missing part of the story of the fall of the house of Amarna. Where the survivors ended up after they fled Saqqara, will no doubt be left other Egyptologists to unearth.

6. https://en.wikipedia.org/wiki/Thutmose_(sculptor)

CHAPTER *11*

# BREAKING THE CODE

Ancestry of two mummies from the Amarna era
discovered in a tomb in the Saqqara Necropolis:
Are they the consort and son of Nefertiti?
Abrahams R, Awass Z, Johansen I, et al,
Nature (2020) volume 105, September 1st
(Abstract and discussion)

## Abstract

The New Kingdom in ancient Egypt, comprising the 18th, 19th, and 20th dynasties, spanned the mid-16th to the early 11th centuries BC. The late 18th dynasty, which included the reigns of pharaohs Akhenaten and Tutankhamun, together with Nefertiti acting as regent, was an extraordinary time. The pharaoh Akhenaten, who ruled from circa 1351 to 1334 BC, is considered one of the most controversial of the Egyptian pharaohs, because his attempt to radically transform traditional religion affected all facets of society and caused great turmoil. The identification of a number of royal mummies from this era, the exact relationships between some members of the royal family and causes of death have been matters of debate.

## Objectives

To use new techniques of molecular and medical Egyptology, to determine familial relationships amongst two out of three mummies of the New Kingdom, that have just been discovered in the necropolis at Saqqara and their cause of death.

## Design

These mummies underwent detailed anthropological, radiological, and genetic studies as part of the King Akhenaten Family Project. Mummies including those from Tutankhamun's immediate lineage served as the genetic and morphological reference. To authenticate DNA results, analytical steps were repeated and independently replicated in a second ancient DNA laboratory staffed by a separate group of personnel. Eleven royal mummies dating from circa 1410–1324 BC and suspected of being kindred of Akhenaten and, including two of Nefertiti's daughters, Meritaten and Meketaten and 5 other royal mummies dating to an earlier period, circa 1550–1479 BC, were examined. In addition, a search was made for genetic material that might suggest their cause of death.

## Main Outcome Measures

Microsatellite-based haplotypes in the mummies, generational segregation of alleles within possible pedigree variants, mRNA and Y chromosome haplotype to suggest matriarchal and patriarchal lineage, archaeological evidence, and their links to the historical record discovered in the binding of the large male. In addition to determine cause of death having excluded trauma.

## Results

Genetic fingerprinting allowed the relationship of these two mummies to the pedigree of Akhenaten's and Tutankhamun's immediate lineage as well as their relationship to Nefertiti. Although the small male carried the mRNA of Nefertiti there was no evidence of him being related to Akhenaten. Confirming that although Nefertiti bore 6 daughters from Akhenaten, this was not his son. Furthermore, re-examining the mRNA of material from Tutankhamun, there was no evidence that he was the son of Nefertiti. The most unexpected finding was the appearance of the Cohen modal haplotype on the Y chromosome of both male cadavers. There was no evidence of trauma, so the assumption is that they died of natural causes. PCR of DNA and RNA fragments at multiple sites in the brain and bone marrow suggested a death from infection with a corona virus.

## Conclusion

Nefertiti and the unknown male were the mother and father of the small male cadaver. This suggests that the third mummy in its casket that is yet to be opened, is that of Nefertiti. We postulate that the two male mummies died from a viral plague. Whether the unknown male is the founder of the Cohen modal haplotype mutation or one of longer lineages, is open to speculation.

## Discussion

To make this discussion more meaningful, it would be an advantage to read the narrative section of Saqqara codex, found on the mummy of the large man, that appeared in the Journal of Egyptian Archaeology on September 1st, 2020.[1] Taking together the translation of this papyrus roll and the molecular and genetic information, provide a clear-cut picture of events taking place 3,500 years ago. The picture will become even more tightly focused when the third of the Saqqara triplets, almost certain to be Nefertiti, has been fully researched. What we can now be said, with near certainty, is that Nefertiti, in the waning years of Akhenaten's rule when she was acting as co-Regent, had a relationship with the court artist, Tuthmose, and gave him two sons, Tuthmoses and Amenhotep. She probably died of breast cancer two years after the death of Akhenaten.

The finding of the Cohen haplotype on the Y chromosomes of both the male corpses indicates that they were amongst the ancestors of the majority of Jewish men today who claim, by oral tradition, to be descendants of the priests from the time of the building the first Temple by King Solomon

---

1. Translation and Interpretation, of a narrative papyrus discovered in the wrappings of a mummy from Amarna period discovered in the necropolis at Saqqara. McCartney A. et al, The Journal of Egyptian Archaeology, Vol. 122, pp 35–52, September 1st, 2020.

in about 1,000 BCE. Molecular evidence currently available, can trace the origin of this mutant Y chromosome back 2,000–3,000 years.[2]

These new observations provide strong evidence that the progenitor of this mutation lived more than 3,300 years ago. Finally, we know that the likely cause of death of both men was from a "plague" of a coronavirus with a similar molecular footprint of the current pandemic of COVID-19.

2. Extended Y chromosome haplotypes resolve multiple and unique lineages of the Jewish priesthood. Michael F. Hammer,1,2 Doron M. Behar,3 Tatiana M. Karafet,1et al. Hum Genet. 2009 Nov; 126(5): 707-717.)

CHAPTER *12*

# SAQQARA, SPRING 2022

T HE pandemic and its impact on foreign travel and social distancing extended well beyond the predictions of the politicians, it even thwarted the best guesses of the mathematical modelers advising the governments of the most developed countries. Although the vaccine scientists were quick to respond and vaccination programmes were already being rolled out in the latter part of 2020, what they hadn't accounted for was the rapid development of variants of the virus. History will record this era as the race between the spread of the virus and the fight back by the brilliant scientists, developing vaccines that could protect the whole global population rather than building anti-viral walls around the wealthy and most developed countries in the world. Ultimately the scientists won the war and the world leant to live with the COVID-19 as with other respiratory virus that are controlled by annual revaccination every winter. Ultimately, most countries in the world had been fully vaccinated and relaxation of the controls for foreign travel and gatherings of mixed communities, were relaxed in the late spring of 2022.

Three days after President Al-Sisi announced the relaxation of the lock-down rules, Prof Sharif decided to have a party in his weekend retreat. The weather had been torrid and the atmosphere in the City where they had been self-isolating, was close to insurrection.

He invited all his children, their spouses and grandchildren, together with his colleagues from his department who were part of the team researching the three mummies. The air at Saqqara was fresher than in the city and a cooling breeze came from the mountains to the west. The family arrived on Friday evening and both his medically qualified sons, Hasan and Abbas, were due for a weekend off duty. The other guests arrived on Saturday morning. They'd enjoyed a quiet day, a light lunch and an afternoon siesta and got together again for a sundowner under the date palms. The red and orange sky peeped through the gaps in the silhouettes of the palm leaves above, as the servants served long glasses of refreshing ice-cold drinks, fruit cocktails for the observant, and chilled beer, gin and tonic or malt whiskey on the rocks for the not so observant. After catching up on everyone's "lock-down" stories, Abdul Sharif embarked on a discussion of their findings before the time of the plague. They were all aware of the remarkable story described in the Codex and the mutually supportive scientific observations of the molecular assays of the material retrieved from the skeleton and hair follicles. The publication of these findings had captured the world's attention and there was pressure from the highest authorities in the land to complete the unveiling of the mysterious white capsule that almost certainly carried the mummified remains of Nefertiti. This alone might be sufficient to kickstart the dormant tourist trade of Egypt now that the pandemic was controlled. This meeting was more than a celebration of the end of lockdown but the first of its kind to plan the next phase in their research of the Saqqara trio from where they left off.

Having agreed where and when to start and planned a zoom meeting with their British counterparts, Ingrid Johansen stepped in with another unresolved mystery. "We can now be sure who the author of the parchment was and his relationship with the mummies. We can speculate that in some ways their flight from Amarna to Saqqara, is linked to the Biblical story of the Exodus, but what happened next? If the legend is based on real facts, then how did they make the journey to the Red Sea, across the Nile and about 100 miles of mountainous desert?" To everyone's surprise, Hasan, their host's oldest son, came up with an answer that had them in thrall. They had forgotten that Dr Hasan Sharif had studied archaeology as his first degree and then trained as a doctor in the hope that he might replace his father as Professor of Anatomy. As it turned out he became so engrossed in the clinical care of sick children, that he ended up as a paediatrician. His PhD thesis was a study of protozoal diseases, like amoebiasis or giardiasis, amongst the most common diseases that are related to contaminated water, that take their toll amongst children under five living close to the Nile Delta. This chance combination of interests allowed him an insight into this specific question. He knew a lot about the geography and history of the

Nile Delta. "Just humour me a little." He started with a smile. "Let me read the last sentence of the translation from the papyrus wrapped around the 'daddy mummy'. '*But first, we must find a way of crossing to the other side of the great river, nay the Red sea, that has sustained the lives of generation after generation to the beginning of time thanks to the will and blessing of our Lord, the Aten*'. I think there is an error here. The word for red is *suph*, that is also the word for reed. In ancient times the Nile delta was referred to as the Reed Sea. I don't believe the fugitives were making for the Red sea, that doesn't make sense. I think they were intent on crossing the Canopic branch of the Nile delta, the only significant obstacle on the route to the flatlands along the southeast corner of the Mediterranean, and then north along the Sinai desert to the land of the Canaanites."

After a pause, everyone nodded in assent. He then continued. "Furthermore, I think I know where the evidence for this assertion, can be found!"

Professor Sharif was very proud of his sons and they all shared the same impish sense of humour. So, after a short interlude of laughter all around, he stood up and announced; "Very funny Hasan, now let's go into dinner." As they stood up and made for the alfresco dining area, Hasan took his father's elbow and whispered, "Baba, I was being serious, hear me out after dinner."

After dinner when most others had gone to bed, Abdul Sharif, his two sons together with Ingrid Johansen, sat outside looking up to a star-lit sky dominated by the Cassiopeia constellation, drinking little cups of sweet black coffee. In ancient Greek mythology, Cassiopeia boasted that she and her daughter Andromeda were more beautiful than all the Nereids, the nymph-daughters of the sea god Nereus. This brought the wrath of Poseidon, the ruling god of the sea, upon the kingdom of Ethiopia. With Nefertiti on their minds, their world seemed dominated by powerful and beautiful women.

After a pause as they enjoyed the pristine atmosphere of the moment, Hasan picked up on what he was saying before dinner.

"Baba, if I'm allowed to proceed let me explain why I think I know where the evidence for the crossing of the *Reed* sea lies buried." His father nodded approval in a manner that suggested scepticism. "In my year at medical school, I built up friendships with three other guys who shared the same cadaver in the dissecting room. We all grew moustaches and called ourselves the four *moustachers*. One of these friends is Kareem Yacoub, who is now head of A&E at Abu Hummus general hospital. Shortly before the lockdown we had a reunion party to mark 20 years from graduation. Like all doctors, we exchange tales about interesting cases we treated. He described how one of his patients, an eccentric Englishman, involved in the sub-aqua archaeological excavations just off the coast east of Alexandria, was caught up in the tsunami of September 2019 and survived after he had been driven down the Canopic branch of the delta nearly 40 Km. All he suffered was a broken ankle. The local villagers at Naucratis, took care of him and brought him to see Kareem. His leg was put in a cast for nearly three months but instead of flying home on the 30th of January like other English guests, he elected to stay. When he came back to have the cast removed the English man told Kareem that he had seen the remains of ancient Egyptian chariots exposed by the tidal wave, shortly before he resurfaced, he even marked the spot with a buoy. This spot is surely on the direct line our refugees would take from here to Ismailia and the northern seaboard of Sinai."

His father could barely supress his excitement. "Hasan dear boy, there is an old saying amongst Egyptologists. 'We make our discoveries not by chance but when the gods of the ancient Egyptians elect', I think this is such a time and we must not ignore the call of the Aten. It is only 70 Km from here to Abu Hummus, I think we should pay this eccentric Englishman a call tomorrow morning!"

David Goddard had "gone native" since the lockdown. He grew his hair long and even had a luxuriant beard until Aisha, his new wife, issued an ultimatum, "either that beard goes, or I go." The beard was shaved off the very same day. He wore a long thaub and thongs on his feet. He loved helping with the harvesting, fishing and sailing on the Nile but most of all he loved being a close member of a small community or clan. He had never before experienced this kind of kinship. He had liquidated all his assets in England via agents and bank transfers and had just sold his two-bedroom flat in west Hampstead for £750,000. What with that and his bank savings he was now a millionaire. In terms of his immediate needs were concerned, it was like he had inherited a fortune. The first thing he did was to pay for the school fees for Ahmed, his adopted son, at the best private boarding school in Alexandria for the new term that started in September that the pandemic was controlled. The next thing he had in mind now the lock down rules had been relaxed, was a visit to Alexandria to recharge his air tanks and buy a couple of spares. He was determined to dive in the Nile and dig around the point where he had resurfaced nearly three years ago.

At 11.00am on that May Sunday morning, he was sitting quietly enjoying his coffee and hookah pipe whilst playing backgammon with Ahmed in what passed for the village square, when they heard the roar of motor vehicles turning off the main road to the bumpy lane leading to the village. This was such a rare event that Ahmed, jumped up and ran towards the village entrance. He arrived just in time to see a jeep and a silver Mercedes appear from amongst the date palms. He rushed back to where he had been seated before and shouted, "Baba, you must hide I think the police and immigration officers have come for you!" Without a second thought the two of them ran towards the ancient ruins of Naucratis to hide in what remained of the catacombs. After about 20 minutes Aisha came searching for them. "David and Ahmed where are you hiding? Come out, come out, wherever you are, some very important people have come to visit you and mean no harm."

They popped their heads out of a hole in the ground like a pair of frightened meerkats that had Aisha bursting out with laughter. "Come out you timid bunnies, the professor of Archaeology from Cairo university, Abdul Sharif, is paying you a courtesy visit."

There is camaraderie amongst scientists who share the same interests. It's almost like being a member of a faith community or the relationships with cousins in an extended family. Once David had overcome his shock at being found in such a remote place and the fear that these strangers were not from the immigration department or worse still the secret service, he settled down quickly to enjoy the company of such a distinguished band of brothers. They hunkered down on whatever box or lump of sandstone that played the role of a chair and were served coffee and sweetmeats by Aisha whose beautiful eyes were sparkling, equally thrilled as her new husband, by these unexpected visitors. Once all introductions were complete, professor Sharif then launched into a long monologue describing the unearthing of the three mummies, the initial anatomical and radiological findings, the DNA/RNA results and finally the translation of the codex. He was heard out with rapt attention from David and Aisha who were soon joined by

Ahmed and after the word had got around, about half of the population of the village. By the time he had finished, David was at threat of wetting his pants with excitement. He immediately asked Ahmed to run and fetch the throwing stick that he had fished out of the water. He came panting back within two minutes, and with a bow passed it on to the famous professor. Abdul Sharif and Ingrid Johansen looked at it closely with the naked eye and the magnifying glasses they always carried with them. Ingrid looked up first with a big smile and addressed herself to Ahmed, "You are a very clever and brave young man for discovering this priceless relic. If it is handed over to the department of antiquities, you will receive a significant sum of money as a reward. This is a very rare artefact and the best specimen I've ever seen. There is no doubt that this belonged to a member of King Tutankhamen's militia from about 1,300 BC, if there is more like this below the sediment of the river at this point, then your father has discovered a treasure trove." Ahmed blushed with pleasure and with a grin on his face made obeisance to the lovely pale lady from the north.

It took them little time to agree how to proceed. Professor Sharif would use all his authority and all his network, that happen to include his cousin, the director of the department of antiquities, to put together a team to conduct a sub-aqua excavation of the Nile basin at this site. They would need two buddy teams to work in shifts and of course David would be in one of these teams. They would have to cut a trench in the sediment below and that would require a high-powered water dredge. The depth of the river at this point was about 10 metres but it sloped quite steeply to the river edge. It was agreed that they start the trench at the river edge and work outwards in a westerly direction. This way, they deduced, if there was a company of charioteers chasing the fugitives, they would chance on finding those at their vanguard. They would need a large supply of air tanks and other equipment. All this would cost money, but Abdul Sharif waved that concern away. "Let me worry about that later. I have another cousin who is the chairman of one of Cairo's biggest private banks, who owes me a favour." With that the visitors returned to their vehicles and sped off in a cloud of dust leaving little time for the natives of the village to take it all in. Ahmed broke the silence; "Ummi, can I buy a motorbike with the money I get in exchange for the boomerang?" Aisha responded with a smile on her face, "No habibi, you can't buy a motorbike but you can buy new trainers, trendy jeans, a leather bomber jacket and anything else that will get the girls swooning over you at your posh school in Alexandria." That seemed to satisfy the young man who skipped off to tell his buddies about the change in his fortunes.

Naucratis had not experienced and invasion like this since the visit of the Assyrians in 676 BC. The vanguard of the column was a camouflaged military van bearing a huge generator and the rest of the kit for sucking out the sands of time. Next came the silver Mercedes bearing Abdul Sharif, Ingrid Johansen and the French husband and wife team of radiologists.

They were followed by a Jeep carrying four tough-looking men wearing keffiyeh casually around their necks, towing a large two-wheeled container. They were the sub-aqua team with all their gear, including a compressor for refilling their air tanks. Taking up the rear was a large campervan that would provide overnight accommodation for the diving team whilst the leaders of the expedition spent their nights in the comfort of the Travel Lodge in Abu Hummus. The villagers poured out of their huts, the dogs went hysterical, a camel broke the cords of its hobble and galloped away chased by two boys, the goats took fright and tried to climb the trees and even a flock of the sacred white Ibis of the Nile took flight to add to the confusion.

Working with military precision, the team of divers unloaded their equipment onto wheeled platforms and trundled them down as close to the banks of the Nile not hidden in the bulrushes. Unknown to the onlookers, the sub-aqua team were in fact a squad of frog men from the Egyptian military unit that gave Israel a fright during the Yom Kippur war of 1973.

One hour later the giant electric generator roared into life. David and one of the frogmen pulled on their wetsuits and shouldered up their air tanks and were soon ready to go but it was agreed that Ahmed, wearing a snorkel mask would lead them as close as possible to the site where he found the throwing stick that had been marked by moving David's buoy a little deeper into the Nile. The NCO of the diving team signalled all was ready and Ahmed dived into the water like a flying fish whilst David and his buddy performed clumsy back flicks into the river shortly afterwards. Within one minute, Ahmed and one of the divers resurfaced leaving David behind. The giant suction tube was dragged to the river edge and the anonymous diver dragged into the water behind him along with two shovels.

After another few minutes a great gurgling noise could be heard on the riverbank and at once the effluent of water, sand and gravel, spewed out around the feet of the cluster of onlookers who got too close to the action.

Compared with the animation on the ground, everything underwater was quiet, calm and controlled. The two divers, having cut into the sloping banks of the river, pulled the duckbill of the dredge into the gap, and started scooping up large mouthfuls of sediment from the riverbed. When they were only two metres from their first cut, they had the first find. At first, they thought it was a broken branch from an overhanging tree, but pulling it up together with a squelch, out popped a bronze spike the sharp end of a spear. They gave the thumbs-up signal to each other and David took the first digital picture of the day. The more they sucked and shovelled the more the evidence grew that a small fighting unit had drowned at that spot. Two hours flew by until the alert that they need to get back on land. With two spearheads, one boomerang-like throwing stick and one sinuous piece of laminated wood, probably the shaft of a compound bow, tied to their belts, they rose to the surface to be received like conquering heroes. The next pair jumped in and continued to work the trench and it wasn't long before they came across the ruins of a chariot. The lightweight and sturdy chariots that were introduced to the Egyptians by the Asiatic Hyksos during the early 18th Dynasty, were constructed of bent wood and leather and often overlaid with gold foil and decorated with cloisonné inlay. Here they stumbled on three examples tangled together. Most of the wood had rotted and the leather was hanging in strips from the remains of the cockpit, but the spokes and elaborate wheels survived having been built with elm and fitted with rawhide tyres.

For the rest of that day and the next, the two by two buddy teams worked their shifts until dusk. They paused on the third day to take a tally of their hoard. The inventory so far suggested that at least five of the chariots in the van of the chase had been recovered together with enough bows, arrows, spears and throwing sticks to supply at least 10 armed men.

They had also identified and photographed the skeletal remains of this troop, together with remnants of their armour. But these remains would be left until their number were increased by experts in dealing with human remains. But the most astonishing find, had no military connotations, yet in its way confirmed their interpretation of the events of more than three thousand years in the past. This was the remains of a small leather pouch with a purse string tie that contained objects of gold inlaid with red carnelian stones and lapis lazuli. These items were bracelets, neck chains, scarabs and other fashionable costume jewellery of some very rich woman in the past. They looked like a matching set but what was so important was the iconography they bore. There was the deer on hind legs, a beetle and a falcon pendant with a carnelian stone solar disc on their heads, a pectoral with a falcon winged scarab and a solar disc on its head and most important, a signet ring of gold with a deep cut cartouche suggesting a link to the family of Akhenaten. These items were not the loot of the militia but the inadvertent loss of the family jewels by a terrified woman running for her life.

At last professor Sharif and his team had proof of their suspicions that this was an exodus from Egypt of a band of monotheist heretics on their way to another land.

# CHAPTER *13*

# THE WOMAN IN WHITE
# OCTOBER 2022 CAIRO

E GYPTIAN history and culture have fascinated people the world over for centuries, but in the 19th century, the Victorian elite took things to a whole new level with "mummy unwrapping" parties. Mummy unwrapping parties would take place soon after the traveller's return from Egypt. Hosts would send out invitations and guests inclined to attend what was sure to be *the* social event of the season would come in droves to see the mummy. Of course, the event itself would be quite smelly but as the mummy unwrapping would take place after dinner and drinking, some might not have "the stomach for it". Some of these mummy unwrapping parties would take place in public settings so that more than just the affluent could behold what lay beneath the mummy fabric. Presumably, it eventually dawned on Victorians that unwrapping mummies and treating human bodies as entertainment was perhaps not the best way to preserve or even appreciate a given culture, especially for purposes of scientific inquiry. Thus, mummy unwrapping eventually fell out of favour with the public and scientists alike. These days when mummies are unwrapped, it is by carried out by a team of well qualified Egyptologists in an academic setting, such as the small anatomy dissecting theatre as found in Cairo's school of medicine.

With the noose of the lockdown in Egypt loosened, the museums and archaeological sites were reopened for tourists, but without reciprocal air bridges and threats of quarantine on returning home, the tourist industry was still in the doldrums. Nevertheless, Professor Sharif thought it was about time they planned the scientific unwrapping of the lady in the white coffin. It wasn't until late September before his British collaborators would be able to re-join his team. Leave of absence from their Universities and opening up an airbridge between London and Cairo delayed matters until October the 10th. In addition to the original team they had a newcomer, David Goddard, who had earnt his place by discovering the precise spot where the putative "Children of Israel" crossed the Reed Sea on dry land that appeared for a short space of time as an adumbration of the tsunami that was to follow. The remains of a squadron of Tutankhamen's, who timed their crossing a few minutes behind the fugitives, was proof enough and to some extent supported the Biblical narrative.

The anatomy dissecting theatre was a D shaped room with walls covered in mahogany wood giving it a sinister atmosphere. It was built in the late 19thC to accommodate students training to be surgeons. The flat wall of the D used to carry a blackboard for the lecturer to scratch diagrams in chalk. These days it carried a huge, touch-sensitive, flat-screen monitor.

The semi-circular walls with tiers of four levels allowed students to see what was going on over their classmates' shoulders protected by a padded bar to lean on in case they came over faint. There were no seats as the professors in the old days believed that students were more alert if kept standing up. On the first day of the unwinding of the lady in white, this viewing area was occupied by technicians and producers from National Geographic. There had been a bidding war to film the proceedings as the potential audience could be counted in millions. National Geographic outbid the BBC, Sky and even Fox News, to win the exclusive rights. Professor Sharif had no misgivings about the probity of the affair as long as the final cut was educational and free of sensationalism. The fact that the fees would support his department and the school of medicine for the foreseeable future was of course a secondary concern. His colleagues from London and Leeds would also get a cut to support their work in the future.

As well as the flat screen monitor on the front wall, two other free-standing versions were placed on each side of the room. On a gantry above, there were video cameras and the business end of the digital X-ray equipment. Standing in the bull ring awaiting the grand entrance of the lady in the white casket were Zahi Awass, Abdul Rashid, Ingrid Johansen, Cecile and Jean Baptiste Du Toit, Robert Abrahams, Lucy Carpenter 'Angus McCartney and David Goddard.

There were other technicians on stand-by who mingled with the National Geographic crew on the steps of the tiered amphitheatre. They were the first to gasp at the beautiful proportions and pristine state of the papier mâché casket as it was rolled in by two other technicians.

The coffin was lifted gently onto the operating table, that as well as being fully adjustable carried X-ray sensitive plates beneath and others that could be slid up along the side for transverse lateral images. As they knew that the mummy was wrapped in radio-opaque material, so the first task was to cut a line around the circumference of the casket and lift off the lid before further studies were possible.

A technician with a small circular saw, cut along the line agreed by the professors as the likely position of the seal linking the bottom and top half of the coffin. Considering it was made with humble papier mâché it was very hard to cut through probably because of the resins in the paste. As the top half was carefully lifted by tapes at each end linked to pullies hanging from the gantry, the lecture theatre was filled with a sighing "Ahhh", from all the witnesses in unison. The head and shoulders were covered with a golden death mask joined to a pectoral of breath-taking beauty that matched that of the boy king Tutankhamen. The face was of a beautiful woman, with pouting ruby lips and high cheekbones hardly disguised by the false beard, the token of her regency. The gold and lapis lazuli from the pectoral plate extended into the crossed arms with the right hand holding a flail and the left holding a crook. Both flail and crook were decorated with blue stripes of lapis. The lower half of her body was covered with flexible gold foil covered in beautifully etched vertical hieroglyphics. Prominent near the region of the right ankle, embedded into the gold was a block of lapis carrying the cartouche of Nefertiti. As that was pointed out a cheer went up from the audience.

The next steps in the extrication of the wrapped mummy from its double carapace of the coffin and the golden shell embellishing were technically difficult. The remains of the cadaver within the linen bandages might be very fragile and in part a husk that could crumble into dust before there was a chance to photograph or X-ray the mummified remains. They had already perfected a new process that in practice was simplicity itself. This involved sliding lubricated six inched tapes at short intervals along the length of the mummy taking special care not to flex the neck. To achieve this, they first had to slide in flexible rods, similar to those used by plumbers to unblock drains. They would then be clipped to the tape that was then pulled to the other side. These tapes would all be linked to pullies on the gantry above so that the wrapped mummy could be lifted sufficiently to allow the lower half of the casket to be removed to join its top half that had been lifted off before. The mummy could then be lowered on to the operating table. Having achieved that with success they realised they had found an unexpected bounty, in that the whole of the interior of the coffin was inscribed with perfectly unblemished hieroglyphics. Angus McCartney could hardly believe his luck.

Next, they removed the gold plates from the torso and then freed the golden mask from the head using heated spatula to melt the resins beneath.

Then the unwrapping procedures began. As it happened it was just as well they took so much trouble in lifting the mummy out of its casket as the outer wrappings crumbled at a touch and became increasingly powdery the closer they were to the body yet the team was able to determine the way in which the body had been wrapped in 16 layers of linen. Care had obviously been taken since each finger and toe had been wrapped separately and fitted with an individual gold cover. The internal organs had been removed through an embalming incision which ran in a horizontal direction from the navel across to the left hip rather than conforming to the standard position in which the incision is made vertically down the left side of the abdomen. The body cavity had been filled with resin-soaked linen which had set rock hard and the skin was brittle. The Queen had been buried wearing gold sandals and an anklet above her right foot and as they worked their way up the remnants of the linen wrapping they found more and more jewellery and by the time they reached her folded arms over the chest they discovered a large golden scarab carrying the sun disc with a ruby on its back with a ruby on the thorax above the heart. Whilst gently uncovering the crossed arms they found them loaded with bracelets from elbow to the wrist. All in all, they recovered nearly 50 items including belts amulets and a large gold signet ring again displaying the cartouche of the queen.

The most striking finding was a necklace with an Udjat Eye Pendant, symbolizing the right eye of the celestial hawk god, Horus. This classic golden talisman, with its enigmatic gaze, was believed to have the power of resurrecting the dead. There was also an elegant gold counterpoise of the necklace, inlaid with cloisonné, representing the hieroglyphic *tyet* sign, a girdle knot symbolizing the protection of Isis.

Leaving the best to last, they turned their attention to the head. Although the skin looked like dried leather, the bone structure was intact. The well-defined cheekbones and her sleeping eyes delineated by long eyelashes gave allusion to her ethereal beauty even three millennia after her death. There was no evidence of a puncture in the skull at the level of her forehead instead they found a gold-encrusted diadem bearing the protective vulture and cobra divinities of Upper and Lower Egypt. Her scalp had obviously been shaven as a sign of her priesthood and was covered by a short-plaited wig. At this point, Lucy Carpenter could no longer restrain her excitement. "It's her, it's her, the very image of the Amarna limestone relief kissing her daughter Meriaten that I described in my PhD thesis." She then broke down in tears.

Once she had regained control of her emotions, she spoke again but with a different tenor to her voice and redirected her gaze from the head to the torso of the dead Queen.

"There's something wrong with her body. The many statues of her created by Tuthmose in the studio at Amarna showed a tall and voluptuous figure. These human remains to measure no more than 4ft 10in length and it looks like she has kyphoscoliosis, or in lay terms, a hunchback. There is no evidence to suggest we fractured the spine in lifting the corpse from its shell, so what's going on?"

"I think I know what's going on." Interjected Cecile Du Toit, "but first we must make the X-rays, n'est-ce pas?"

Within no time at all, the X-rays of the corpse were available for all to see with the digital images displayed on the monitors. It was quite obvious, even to those without medical education, that the cause of her deformity was also the cause of her untimely death. The whole skeleton was riddled with translucencies, which included her cranial bones and the shafts of her femoral bones. These were the stigmata of metastases from cancer, most likely with a primary focus in the breast, the "cold bulging tumour". The hunchback appearance was explained by pathological fractures at the levels of T4-T6 of the thoracic vertebra. She must have died in extreme pain and paralysed below the waist. The only comfort she might have had was to consume opium in large doses that might have mercifully hastened her death. On learning this, Lucy once again broke down in tears whilst at the same time Abdul Sharif got some dust in his eyes and asked to be excused for a short while.

The whole team had much to occupy themselves after this day of utmost drama.

Lucy took care of the wig and samples of individual eyelashes. Robert took care of the remnants of shrunken brain matter from the occipital region of the skull together with samples from the bone marrow cavities. He also took samples from the cavities in the thoracic vertebrae hoping that he might find remnants of the DNA from the cancer cells that killed her. Ingrid Johansen was given the tasks of cataloguing the jewellery and other ornaments collected from the dust of her linen wrappings. Angus, assisted by his wife, took on the Herculean task of recording and translating the scripts on the interior surfaces of the coffin and the gold foil coverings of the mummy's torso. Professor Sharif and his cousin Zahi Awass took custody of the golden mask and pectorals and transported them to a secure place at the Cairo museum already contemplating the income they could make by setting up a special exhibition of their finds. Cecile and Jean Baptiste had plenty to do in examining the bones in detail using a variety of imaging techniques. The only one left empty handed was David Goddard who was in any case anxious to get back to his wife. Just before he left it was agreed they would all meet again in two weeks' time to integrate all the discoveries from each of the specialists together.

Towards the end of the month they reconvened to learn of each other's observations. This time the meeting was held round the large mahogany table in the board room at the medical school where they were served a celebratory lunch. To provide some kind of order to the proceedings, they decided to start from the outside and work their way down to the molecular level. In other words, start with the inscriptions on the inner surfaces of the casket and end up with the genomics.

Angus kicked off by projecting images of the hieroglyphics on the interior surface of the coffin and handed round copies of his translations that he then read out loud.

> *May Aten bless the Great Royal wife his beloved abounding in her perfection She who sends the attend to rest with a sweet voice and her perfect hands bearing two sistrums, the mistress of the two lands, Nefreneferuaten Nefertiti, living forever and ever. May she be by the side of Akhenaten for ever and ever. We kiss the pure ground before her feet. She is the morning star, shining bright, fair of skin lovely the look of her eyes and the sweet the speech of her lips. With upright neck, shining breasts, hair of true lapis lazuli, arms surpassing gold, fingers like lotus buds, heavy thighs yet narrow waist, her legs parade her beauty. With graceful steps she walks, capturing all hearts with her movements, causing all men's heads to turn when they see her. There is joy for him who embraces her when she steps out, she competes with the sun. And may she live side by side with Aten the sun of all who live in this life and the life to come.*

Next he changed the picture on the monitor to the inscription in the wrapping of gold foil. This was a much shorter text but reinforced the adulation inscribed on the queen's coffin.

> *Great one of the Palace, fair of face, adorned in the double plumes, lady of joy at the sound of whose voice the King rejoices, possessor of grace, great of love, whose arrangements please the King, leader of Aten's encourage, who satisfies him as he rises at dawn, everything she says is done, the Great Royal wife, beloved lady of Egypt, Neferneferuaten- Nefertiti may she live forever.*

Angus had little to say after his recitation as the text needed no explanation or elaboration but mentioned the possibility that the golden wrapping might have been inscribed in anticipation of her death rather than post-mortem.

Next up was Ingrid who delighted the assembly with beautiful high-resolution images of each of the queen's jewels and amulets. Their combined value on the open market might be close to the GDP of Sudan but they would never be sold and would look wonderful displayed in vitrines under blue light at the exhibition they were already planning. *En passant* she mentioned that for a monotheist there were a remarkable number of emblems linked to the multitudes of minor gods and goddesses in the pantheon of ancient Egypt.

Abdul Sharif then showed his pictures of the golden bejewelled death mask and breastplate.

He then showed a "photoshopped" 3D image of the mask without the ceremonial beard and compared it with the famous bust of Nefertiti in the Neues museum in Berlin. The resemblance was uncanny. The craftsmanship was of the same quality as that for the death mask of King Tut.

Lucy had little to add to her speciality but confirmed that the queen's wig was of the design and quality of a high priestess. With a grin directed at Robert, she claimed the credit for the best source of DNA in the papillae of the eyelashes she'd plucked from the lady's upper eyelid.

Cecile and Jean Baptiste reviewed all the X-rays they'd already seen together with new magnified images and scans from an open bodied CT contraption. One of their new discoveries was additional amulets hidden in the thoracic cavity and packed in amongst the solidified linen bundles in the abdominal cavity.

Last but not least, Robert Abrahams took the stage and ran through the esoteric details of his studies of the nuclear and mitochondrial DNA that confirmed what they already knew, that this mummy was indeed the mother of the young man whose mummy accompanied hers to the pit in Saqqara. In addition, it was clear that her genome had much in common with the well-studied DNA of her oldest daughter, Meritaten. Then like a magician pulling a rabbit out of a hat, he described a remarkable observation in the DNA from the papilla of one of the Queen's eyelashes. "On a hunch, I made a specific search for sequences that are linked to the cytogenetic location: 17q21.31, which is the long arm of chromosome 17 at position 21.31. And sure enough, I found the mutation I was looking for. In case you haven't guessed so far this is the oldest example of the BRCAI ever reported. We have long speculated that the founder mutation dated back more than 3,000 years and that its origins were in the Near East, but this is the confirmation we hoped for. As you know these BRCAI mutations are associated with a risk of developing breast cancer of a virulent phenotype at a relatively young age. We call it one of the Ashkenazi mutations although it can be found amongst the Mizrachi Jews who came out of Babylon. It could only have found its way into the Jewish population at large if this couple, Nefertiti and Tuthmose, had passed it on to their son, the one responsible for writing the Saqqara codex. Indirectly I think I have the answer to the earlier question posed by Ingrid. The paradox of the excess of treasure and the iconography of polytheism hidden in the wrappings with the puritanical appearance of the coffin. I suggest that when Nefertiti died many fans wanted to be sure she entered the afterlife in style and decided to cover all bases so as not to offend any overlooked gods or goddesses. After her death, we witness the emergence of fundamentalism in the surviving generation that wiped every human feature from the surface of the porcelain white coffin. Speaking as the only Jew in this happy crew I'm not the least surprised. I've had many confrontations with the extreme right-wing of my coreligionists. As a scientist, I define myself as a Spinoza brand of Jew and that makes me a heretic in their opinion. It wouldn't bother me if they kept to their beliefs and practices in the confines of their closed communities, but in some parts of the USA and in Israel, they have become very powerful and extended their influence in a way that finds common purpose with the anti-Semites. The fact that we've just witnessed the birth of monotheism that in one generation has given birth to fundamentalism, is remarkable but not surprising."

On that note, the meeting broke up as they prepared themselves for a celebratory party in professor Sharif's compound that saw the start of this adventure.

CHAPTER *14*

# A MEETING OF MINDS

I LANDED at terminal 5, London Heathrow (LHR) on time, excited to be reunited with my wife and daughter. Angus and Lucy took a later flight to Manchester that was much nearer their home. As I exited with my bags in the arrival hall, there were Sophie and Chloe at the barrier waving frantically to catch my attention. They were not alone but surrounded by journalists and TV crews who appeared to be welcoming a celebrity just behind me. I looked around to see if there were any familiar faces before finally waking up to the reality, that *I* was a celebrity. I later learnt that the National Geographic computers had been hacked and clips from the film of the unveiling of Queen Nefertiti had already appeared on the news channels the previous evening. After hugs and kisses from my wife and daughter, I had to battle my way through the morass of the press with padded microphones and cameras being shoved in my face. I recognise that I'm something of an exhibitionist and not shy of controversy, but this was frightening. "The curse of the Pharaohs" took on another meaning.

In the end, if only to protect my family from being trampled to death, I stopped and turned around and made a short speech, "Ladies and gentlemen of the press, thank you for this very warm welcome. I bring you greetings from ancient times and my agent has prepared a statement from the archaeological team who discovered the mummy of Nefertiti". At this point I nodded at a complete stranger standing by my side, and whilst the attention of the media was distracted, ducked down and herded Sophie and Chloe to the limo that was waiting to pick us up at the door. As we sped off with the hounds of the paparazzi on our heels, we fell about laughing but not for long.

We live in Stanmore on the north west margin of greater London and it takes about 45 minutes by car from LHR to get home. As we turned into the cul-de-sac, we were alarmed to find it full of strangers and blocked by vans carrying the logos of the top TV companies in town together with aliens from France and Japan. With much hooting and at the risk of manslaughter, the Uber taxi managed to drop us off in the drive. The baying mob then descended on my little family at the doorstep. Fortunately, our neighbours disturbed by the crowd, had already called the police. Within a minute or two a couple of squad cars with flashing lights and sirens, drove through the crowd with less concern about knocking over the troublemakers than my kindly Uber driver. The head of the squad, inspector Troy, a friend of mine from the golf club, leapt out of the first car and with a megaphone told everyone to behave nicely, or words to that effect. He was rewarded by a heart melting smile from my wife as we were safely escorted indoors.

I was shaking by this time and needed a double scotch to calm my nerves. My daughter was delighted having posed for photographs whilst I was struggling to fit my keys in the lock. Her standing amongst her school friends would certainly rise if she made the front pages of the Daily Mail the next morning. She could already see the headlines, "Professor's daughter, Chloe Abrahams, looks the double of Queen Nefertiti, discovered by her father".

Once I had calmed down and unpacked it was time for Deliveroo to ring the doorbell and deliver three pizzas. As we sat down to our humble supper the enormity of these developments sunk in and I started having morbid thoughts about the fate of Lord Carnarvon and Howard Carter. Sophie, the wise member of the family, suggested how I might manage this exposure to publicity. She reminded me that I was an academic first and foremost, not a Hollywood film star and that I should seek the advice of the public relations team at UCL.

I then trotted off to my study to prepare an e-mail to this effect. I fired up my iMac and launched the Mail App. To my dismay I found my in-box swamped with over 100 messages, most of them hate mail and three of them threatening harm and one with the chilling words, "we know where you live". Amongst this garbage was one from the University that seemed to have pre-empted Sophie's advice. The Provost's PA was politely requesting my presence in his office the next morning at 10.30 am. In a completely

different way, these words were also chilling. When the Provost was polite you knew you were in deep water. I chose not to inform my wife and
daughter of those threats but before turning in, I sent an e-mail to Inspector
Troy, thanking him for his intervention and asking for his advice about the
death threats.

The next morning, I chose to take the tube to UCL for fear of being held
up in traffic and being late for my meeting with the Provost. That involved
taking the Jubilee line to Bond Street and changing to the Central line to
Tottenham Court Road which was a short walk to Gower Street and the
main University campus. Along the way, I had strange looks from other
passengers who were obviously trying to place my face amongst the thousand demi-gods that filled the pages of magazines like "Hello". I arrived
in good time in the outer office of the principal of UCL and was warmly
welcomed by Mrs Penelope Granger, the grey-haired wolf at the door protecting her master from unwanted visitors. On this occasion, her welcome
was almost warm. Instead of the traditional humiliating wait, I was shown
into the inner sanctum with no delay. Standing up to greet me for a group
of five all wearing smiles on their faces.

Sir Arthur Penrose, OM, FRS, Provost of the University, shook my
hand vigorously as did the Dean of my faculty, Ambrose Goodenough, although his smile looked a bit forced. I was then introduced to Kylie Craig, a
glamorous blond woman with scarlet lipstick who apparently was the chief
of media and public affairs at the National Geographic organisation.

The fourth person in the room was vaguely familiar and was intro-
duced as Professor Michael Fallowfield, Vice Provost and head of UCL
Enterprise, the business wing of the university. And last but not least was
Sir Bernard Fisher, director of the nearby British Museum.

I was invited to sit down and offered coffee and a chocolate biscuit.
Clearly, I was not about to be suspended again but I was not expecting what
came next.

Sir Arthur opened the proceedings. "Professor Abrahams, may I be
the first to congratulate your most remarkable discoveries. It appears that
you have not just discovered the long-lost mummy of Nefertiti but have
discovered something even more important. You and your colleagues seem
hell-bent on rewriting the Biblical story of the Exodus. All this has been

leaked following the hacking of the National Geographic computers and Miss Craig assures us that they have discovered the miscreants and you are in no way to blame." At that point, Miss Craig nodded and gave me a smile and a wink. "What we want to do is to exploit this unfortunate occurrence in an opportunistic way. I tell you in absolute confidence, that like many of the Russell Group of Universities, we are facing a crisis in funding as a result of the lockdown and the diplomatic row between the UK and China. 30% of our students come from China and their fees were £9,000 a term. We have also lost other investments from China that sustained our engineering and computer science faculties following the government's decision to renege on the Huawei agreement for the development of our 5G telecommunication service. Our neighbours in the British Museum have also been hit hard. They've lost of their paying members and loss of income as a result of cancelling two of their blockbuster exhibitions. With all this in mind, we want to make your name a brand and raise funds from the copyright on all your work and the spin-off by way of media events. You of course will earn a share of the income and we will negotiate similar agreements with the University of Leeds and the University of Cairo. What do you think about these suggestions?" At that point, I repeated my act like a goldfish by opening and closing my mouth without any words being fashioned. "I take that as a yes," said Miss Craig with a twinkle in her eye. "Allow me to suggest a catch-phrase for this initiative. How about 'The Mystery of the Nile Delta'? MOND for short". At that point Sir Bernard Fisher joined in. "We at the BM have agreed to a partnership with UCL that will host an exhibition and a symposium to launch the programme. I've already had a quiet word with the director of the department of antiquities in Cairo and he supports our plans. For the exhibition we will be lent all the findings from the Saqqara triplets and supplement them with objects, artefacts and mummies from our own collection. The exhibition will remain in place for three months and then transferred to Cairo as its permanent home. Dr Awass will be invited to chair the conference in London and in return I will chair the repeat of the event in Cairo. This makes sense because the event in London will draw more people than in Cairo and in any case, we are all equal parties when distributing the profits."

From that point on matters moved at a speed unknown in the Elysian fields of academia. The University was fighting for survival and the partnership between Professor Fallowfield, Kylie Craig, and the director of the BM, had a dynamism I'd never met before. Our friends and colleagues in Egypt and the north of England, easily persuaded their Universities that this was a win-win situation and the Egyptian department of antiquities anticipated a huge surge in tourism for the Cairo museum, Saqqara and Amarna, following this initiative. The events to launch MOND were to be in the weeks leading up to Christmas and the merchandise linked to the event was self-evident. Monday the 14th of December was chosen for the launch and through backdoor negotiation, the Regent Street Traders association had agreed to give the annual Christmas lighting display an Egyptian theme. The angels of the previous year could easily be transformed into the goddess Isis.

I left work early and treated myself to an Uber in my haste to share my good news with Sophie but was alarmed to find inspector Troy accompanied by a shaven-headed tough guy waiting for me. My wife was offering them tea, but I could tell by the rattling of the cups on the saucer and the pallor of her complexion, that all was not well.

Troy jumped up and gave me an ironic salute and introduced me to the stranger who squatted there like an ugly toad. "Robert allow me to introduce my friend, Uri Ginsberg from the Israeli Embassy. Uri and I have shared intelligence from time to time and although he looks like a Doberman Pinscher is actually a pussy cat." Mr Ginsberg's face was softened by a wide smile as he leapt up and gave me a bone-crushing handshake. "Professor Abrahams, it is an honour to meet you in the flesh." Much to my surprise he spoke perfect English but with a Manchester accent. "My people at the embassy aided and abetted by your local police force have been keeping an eye on you and your beautiful wife. Mrs Abrahams, of course, has dual nationality and we always care for our own but you Professor, are considered a valuable asset and a potential target. I've already learnt that you've had death threats on Twitter...." Sophie interrupted his flow by screaming at me, "Death threats! Death threats! Why didn't you tell me?" The man whom I assumed, was from Mossad, did his best to calm her down. "Do not fear Mrs Abrahams, all is under control and your husband can easily defuse this threat if he listens very carefully to what I have to say. Now let us sit down and talk things through. I have a message from the Ambassador herself who considers your safety a top priority." At this point, I had to interrupt. "Excuse me, what do you mean by *herself*. As far as I know, the Israeli Ambassador is Mark Regev. I've actually met him a few times."

"Ah but there you are wrong and not up to date. Mr Regev has ended his term in office and was replaced last year by Tzipi Hotovely. To say the least, she is a little to the right-wing of politics compared with Mr Regev. She has just given up her post as Israel's settlement minister and rejects all Palestinian claims to any part of the West Bank, Gaza or East Jerusalem. You can then understand the concerns of the constituency she represents when you try to rewrite the history of the Children of Israel. She has learnt through our own sources, Shin Bet to be precise, that some of the zealots from the settlement group and those who want to rebuild the Third Temple have you in their sights. I see you are fidgeting but do not despair we have a simple solution for you that should not require compromising your scientific integrity. As I understand it your work says nothing about the period between Joseph and his multicoloured dream coat and the Amarna period at the time of the 18th dynasty or after the crossing of the Red Sea, Reed sea, whatever, and Joshua bulldozing the walls of Jericho. Your story has a middle but not a beginning or an end. Can you develop theories that fill in the gaps? I don't expect you to search for more archaeological evidence one way or another, but come up with some ideas that might placate our over-zealot brethren?"

Whilst I was being distracted by this terrifying discourse, Chloe had arrived back from school and slipped into our sitting room and heard what had just been saying. She burst into tears and threw herself into my arms. That settled it for me. "Mr Ginsberg, to hell with my scientific integrity, the safety of my wife and daughter trumps all other considerations. Don't worry about my public presentation of the fruit of my labours amongst the dead of ancient Egypt, if necessary, I will evoke miraculous interventions by Ha'Shem to explain our findings to protect the lives of my loved ones in northwest London!" The Mossad man nodded with a sympathetic expression on his face and held his hand up with the palm facing me. "Thank you for hearing me out and understanding the gravity of the situation. Whilst this matter is being sorted out you will be under our covert attention. Here is my card, call me any time 24/7 if you feel threatened in any way but please, I beg of you, try and come up with a manuscript of what you intend to say at the opening of the symposium on the 14th of December within the week."

"How on earth did you know that the meeting was on the 14th of December? We only decided that a few hours ago!"

"We have our eyes and our ears everywhere Professor and it might not surprise you that one of our agents was present at your meeting. That in itself should provide some comfort"

Leaving me dumbfounded, Mr Ginsberg and inspector Troy, took their leave.

CHAPTER 15

# RABBI COHEN AND
# THE MISSING LINKS

T HAT night we couldn't sleep so at midnight we came back down in
our dressing gowns to drink hot chocolate and reprise the events of
the day. The demand made of me was something I couldn't manage
on my own, as my Biblical historicity was not up to the task, but it was
my daughter who came up with the obvious solution. Chloe was in the 6th
form of the Jewish Free School and her best friend was Suzanne Cohen the
daughter of our Rabbi, the reverent doctor Isaac Cohen. Although I didn't
attend the Stanmore synagogue very often apart from the High Holydays
in September and October, if I had nothing better to do on Shabbat, I
enjoyed popping in to hear his sermons. Although the community were
orthodox and aligned with the United Synagogues of Great Britain and
the Commonwealth, Isaac Cohen was very tolerant and enjoyed debating
philosophical issues when we met at social functions, weddings and bar
mitzvahs. His sermons and his books on moral philosophy were scholarly
as well as entertaining. No fire and brimstone more virtue as its own reward. His doctorate from Jews College, a faculty at UCL, was on the subject
of the lost tribes of Israel so it seemed logical to ask him about the tribes
before they got lost.

The next morning, I phoned him up to see if we could have coffee
together when he was free to discuss a very confidential matter. I suspect he
thought I wanted to confess adultery or something, so in a tone of voice that
sounded like a priest in a confessional, he invited me round for 11.00 that

same morning. I was greeted at the door by his lovely bubbly wife, Anita, and ushered into their modest living room where Rabbi Cohen sat amidst a ziggurat of volumes of the Talmud together with the novels "Angels & Demons" and "Inferno" by Dan Brown. He gave me a warm welcome, Anita served us coffee and *kichela* before discreetly backing out. After a sip of coffee and a bite of the Rebbetzin's delicious biscuits, I started telling my story. The Rabbi listened attentively jotting down notes on a yellow legal pad as I spoke but never once interrupting my flow. After I'd finished, he sat quietly looking into the distance in deep thought until I lost patience and broke the silence with the polyvalent Yiddish word of Enquiry, *"Nu?"* He turned to me with a benevolent smile and said.

"I think I have the solution about how we can reconcile your scientific integrity without jeopardising my faith. You have to admit Robert, that was some achievement for any man of the cloth in the five minutes you allowed. The challenge is greater than you think as it is a threefold task. First to fill in the gap between Joseph and your Tuthmose, then to accept that the 10 plagues weren't acts of Ha'Shem but natural happenings and then fill the gap between the crossing of the Red Sea and the conquest of Canaan by Joshua. As lives might be at stake, I think a little compromise on both our accounts is called for but let me reassure you I'm up to the task. Give me 48 hours and in the meantime, I recommend you read the book 'The Exodus' by my friend and colleague Richard Friedman, Professor of Jewish Studies at the University of Georgia. You will learn that amongst other things you are not the first to claim the monotheism of Akhenaten was the precursor of Judaism. Sigmund Freud got there first, let me read you a few lines from his book if I can find it." He stood up and searched his bookshelves before coming up with a slim volume entitled *Moses and Monotheism*. The book was well-thumbed, and he found the passage without difficulty.

"Here it is so listen carefully. *'Now we should have expected that one of the many people who have recognised that Moses is an Egyptian name would also have drawn the conclusion or would at least have considered the possibility that the person who bore this Egyptian name may himself have been Egyptian. Nevertheless, so far as I know no historian has drawn this conclusion in the case of Moses'*. So, you have not shocked me as I have long considered this possibility myself. You can borrow this book as well as my copy of Friedman's book. The task you have set me is welcome above and beyond the demand for the pastoral care of my congregants. I myself face threats of a different kind that I will share with you when we next meet."

We agreed on a time and a date for the following Sunday morning before when he promised to send me a WORD doc of his deliberations by e-mail. He kept his promise and I chose to print it here in full.

***

## From Joseph to Joshua
## 27thC BCE- 13th CBCE

### Joseph

Imhotep lived during the 27th century BCE, in Memphis, Egypt. He was the vizier, architect, astrologer, and chief minister to Djoser who reigned in the years 2630–2611 BCE, as the second king of Egypt's third dynasty. He is considered to have been the architect of the step pyramid built at the necropolis of Saqqara, the oldest extant monument of hewn stone known to the world. Imhotep's high standing in Djoser's court is confirmed by an inscription bearing his name on a statue of Djoser found at the site of the Saqqara pyramid. The inscription lists a variety of titles, including chief of the sculptors and chief of the seers. Although no contemporary account has been found that refers to Imhotep as a practising physician, ancient documents illustrating Egyptian society and medicine during the Old Kingdom (c. 2575– c. 2130 BCE) show that the chief magician of the pharaoh's court also frequently served as the nation's chief physician.

I believe that Joseph and Imhotep were the same person.

The Bible tells us that Joseph was responsible for saving Egypt from a seven-year famine and may have built the massive underground silos that can be found in many cities of Egypt. In particular, he may have built the silos adjacent to the Djoser Pyramid complex at Saqqara. There are many similarities between the profile of Joseph and Imhotep. Imhotep is also credited with saving Egypt from a seven-year famine after hearing of the Pharaoh's dream. Imhotep, like Joseph, was a commoner who was placed second in charge of Egypt by the King. Joseph bought up all the land for Pharaoh by selling the grain he stored during the seven years that preceded the famine; early in Egypt's history and explains how the Pharaohs became so powerful. Until recently, the most compelling argument against Joseph and Imhotep being the same person, has been the discrepancy between the estimated times during which they lived. If the alignment of the Egyptian dynasties is correct, it is highly likely that Joseph and Imhotep were the same person and Egyptian History would be consistent with the Bible. If it can be accepted that Joseph and Imhotep were the same person, this would give historians an anchor in history in order to further correlate the history of Egypt Israel. Going back one generation according to the Bible, Jacob bore 12 sons and a daughter. The eleventh son was Joseph. Joseph was the first son of Rachael, Jacob's second wife. In the Biblical account, (Genesis 37–50) Jacob (Israel) favoured Joseph over his other children. Joseph had a dream that one day he would rule over his brothers. His brothers became jealous of him and so sold him to slave traders who took him to Egypt. He was subsequently sold to Potiphar in Egypt as a slave and was subsequently wrongfully imprisoned. It was in prison where he came to the attention of Pharaoh through his cupbearer who informed Pharaoh of Joseph's ability to interpret dreams by the power of God. Pharaoh needed counsel about his own dreams and was not able to find anybody from his own kingdom to help. Joseph was able to tell Pharaoh the meaning of his dreams which predicted of a coming famine lasting seven years but preceded by seven years of abundance. Pharaoh made Joseph second in charge over his all his kingdom. During the seven years of abundance, Joseph was able to build silos in every city and store enough grain to feed the Nation during the seven years of famine that followed. When Joseph was 30 years old, Pharaoh put him in charge of the whole land of Egypt. Pharaoh gave Joseph his signet ring, dressed him in fine linen and put a gold chain around his neck. He was given a chariot to ride around Egypt as second in command and he was given a wife Asenath, daughter of the priest Potiphera. During the seven years of abundance, Joseph stored up huge quantities of grain in each city from the fields surrounding them. From thereon, the story follows exactly the well-charted history of Imhotep that is carved in stone and inscribed in papyri. The duration of time between the reign of Djoser of the 3rd dynasty and Akhenaten of the18th dynasty is about 1,250 years and it suggested that at some point the princely decedents of Imhotep/Joseph contributed to list of future Pharaohs, Amenhotep I-IV. Amenhotep I (1525–1504 BCE) was followed by Tuthmose I (1504–1492 BCE) suggesting that Tuthmose, the artist of the court at Amarna, was in a direct lineage from Joseph of the Bible.

I love the Biblical story of Moses in the bulrushes but now it takes another meaning as a cover-up to explain a new baby in the household.

*And she put the boy in it and put it in the reeds by the Bank of the Nile and his sister stood still at a distance to know what would be done to him. And Pharaoh's daughter went down to bathe at the Nile and her girls were going alongside the Nile and she saw the Ark amongst the reeds and sent her maid and she took it. And she opened it and saw him. the child: and here was a boy crying, and she had compassion on him, and she said, "this is one of the Hebrews' children". And his sister said to Pharaoh's daughter "shall I go and call a nursing woman from the Hebrews for you and she shall nurse the child for you", and Pharaoh's daughter said to her "Go" and the girl went and called the child's mother and Pharaoh's daughter said to her, "take this child and nurse him for me and I will give you pay." And the woman took the boy and nursed him, and the boy grew older and she brought into pharaoh's daughter and he became her son and she called his name Moses and she said because I drew him from the water. (Exodus 2:3b-10)*

## The 10 plagues

*I will appoint terror over you, consumption and fever, that shall make the eyes to fail and the soul to languish. (Lev. 26:16)*

The whole world is engaged with the current pandemic, with ways to contain it, develop a vaccine, support front-line medical staff, and offer financial relief to the unemployed and to industries and businesses seriously affected by it. A rabbi must struggle hard to avoid the temptation to explain away such theological challenges to faith that have mystified the greatest minds since biblical times, such as why the righteous suffer, why innocent little babies have had their lives snuffed out, not at the hands of the wicked and the violent who defy God's law, but through the power of nature, the very instrument of God's will. We have no explanation. Faith may enable us to cope, but it does not get us beyond the stages of exploration; certainly not disclosure. Faith is a mirror, not a window. If it discloses anything, it is the intensity of the individual's attempt to reach out to his God and to acknowledge the limits of one's own knowledge. It does not guarantee any reciprocal disclosure or moral clarity to an extent that can help make sense of the senseless or shed any light on the mysteries of good and evil, reward and punishment.

At the very beginning of the Torah, we have a description of two worlds. The one, termed *Gan Eden*, is the idyllic, spiritual world of harmony and innocence, where few rules and restrictions were necessary to maintain awareness of God's existence and ownership of the universe. And the other, a physical world outside of that garden: a world of sweat and tears, violence, jealousy, enmity, greed and passion. Adam and Eve were banished from the inner world to the outer. At that point, man was subjected to experiences that reflected more accurately the passion for the physical that he had determined to cultivate when he chose the fruit of the tree rather than the fruit of God's lips. The outer world was riven by turbulence, reflective of the turbulence in man's soul. It was subject to violent physical change, through the effect of nature's laws having already been broken, paving the way to what we describe as "natural disasters" or "acts of God." In the outer world, nature gets its own back for Adam's rebellious seizure of nature's choicest fruit, for his act of plunder of the Tree of the knowledge of good and evil, the repository of lust, violence, and obsession with self. So, according to this view, man, by yearning for the physical experience, was granted his wish, and, with it, a world that is inherently dangerous and turbulent, where the serpent does not commune with Eve but seeks to harm her; where the lion does not lie down with the lamb but seeks to devour it; where nature is largely untamed and unpredictable; and wherein man is as often the vanquished as he is the victor. So, man's eternal struggle with nature is generally of his own making, rather than a threat inherent in nature. And it is against that background that any alleged theological dilemmas relating to our pandemic and similar devastations may be viewed.

I therefore have no problem when you attempt to ascribe the 10 plagues, we recount on first and second nights of Pesach, to natural causes. In addition to the viral pandemic we are facing, there has been a tsunami hitting the Nile delta that would allow men to cross the waters on dry land, a plague of locusts has hit Sudan and upper Egypt, a spill of oil has turned the river Nile red, the oil has killed the fish that live on frog spawn and that has led to a plague of frogs. Others amongst the extreme fundamentalist faction of Judaism, think otherwise and claim that these events are signs from Ha'Shem that we are being punished for our sins and will only achieve redemption if we build the third Temple in Jerusalem and reintroduce animal sacrifice. I will return to this matter at the end of this script.

# From Exodus to the fall of Jericho

Let me first agree with you. I think it highly likely that the Levites were the servants of the Cohanim, not slaves. The Hebrew word *ebed* (עֶבֶד ) can be translated as either slave or servant. I cannot challenge your work on the molecular genealogy of the tribes. Modern orthodox Jews accept the findings of these new scientific methods and I think your explanation of the genomic differences between the priests and their servants is cogent and that also adequately resolves the anomaly about the apportioning the land of Israel amongst the tribes. This then brings me to thinking about the descendants of the other sons of Jacob. If we exclude Levi, but include Ephraim and Manasseh the sons of Joseph, we have 12 tribal lands namely; Reuben, Simeon, Judah, Dan, Issachar, Zebulun, Naphtali, Gad, Asher, Benjamin, Ephraim and Manasseh. I would suggest that in the 1,250 years between Joseph and Moses, without adequate leadership, they would have lapsed into paganism like all their neighbours. I also factor in that Moses' decree of wandering in the desert after the sins of the spies following the Exodus from Egypt, which we read in the *Sedra, Shelach L'cha*, makes no sense. It has always seemed a disproportional sentence for the crime of שְׁנַיִם עָשָׂר הַמְרַגְּלִים (12 spies) when 10 out of the 12 came back with pessimistic predictions for the outcome of a war with the Canaanites. I have a better explanation that will suit both of us with any compromise. The 40 years in the wilderness is a metaphor to describe the period of time between the arrival of Moses and the other Cohanim, that it took to re-educate the tribes in the supreme spiritual worth of monotheism as compared with paganism.

A major issue in the historicity of this period is the narrative of the Israelite conquest of Canaan, described in Joshua and Judges. Most sources now support the biblical narrative of conquest would be affirmed by the archaeological record; and indeed, support the biblical narrative, including excavations at *Beitin* (identified as Bethel), *Tel ed-Duweir*, (identified as Lachish), Hazor, and Jericho.

There is another nuanced clue to support this theory and that is the tribal land of Dan. At the time of Joshua, say between 1250–1200 BCE, the tribe of Dan occupied land with a southern border with Philistia, a western border at the sea in the area covered by Tel Aviv/Jaffa and an eastern border touching the land of Ephraim. Something happened that has never been adequately explained when the tribe of Dan was kicked out of its original homeland in the conquered lands of Canaan and fled to the northernmost tip of ancient Israel which is now in the Hula valley abutting the Lebanese border. Tel Dan is a beautiful archaeological site and a nature reserve with the tributaries of the river Jordan running off mount Hermon into a lake that feeds the mythical river. Here you will find archaeological evidence dating back more than three thousand years of a cultic temple with a sacrificial altar carrying the images of a horned creature. I believe the Danites never adopted monotheism and were driven out from the seashore to the far north by Moses and the army lead by Joshua. It is not difficult to understand that after the death of King Solomon, his son Jeroboam, established his first Temple in Bethel to continue the conventional rituals of the original King Solomon's Temple and his second Temple up north to satisfy the paganism of his tribe. This may be how the story of worshipping the golden calf appears in the book of Exodus and also explains why the prophet Isaiah warned Israel that if they did not repent, the Lord would use Assyria as "the rod of mine anger" (Isaiah 10:5). The tribes of the Northern Kingdom were defeated at the time of the Assyrian conquest in 722 BCE and driven into captivity to be lost until this day. If you don't believe me, drop into the British Museum and look at the bas reliefs from Nineveh.

## Should we rebuild the Temple in Jerusalem?

This is where I need something in return from you although I hope you will judge we share a common purpose. In anticipation of your next visit, I would like you to read this commentary published in *Jewish Political Studies review Volume 11:1–2 (Spring 1999). THE POLITICAL ROLE OF THE ISRAELI CHIEF RABBINATE IN THE TEMPLE MOUNT QUESTION by Yoel Cohen* (See attachment)

The capture by Israel of the Temple Mount in 1967 opened Pandora's box of questions for religious authorities. These ranged from whether to rebuild the Temple and reinstitute the sacrificial service to whether to allow Jews to ascend the Temple Mount to pray. The official Israeli Chief Rabbinate adopted a mostly conservative stance toward the new circumstances created. Halachic factors interplayed with governmental pressure to avoid hostile reactions from the Muslim world. This article examines the approaches of successive chief rabbis to the Temple Mount question, the discussions within the Chief Rabbinate Council, and the social and political contexts in which decisions have been made.

This debate has come to a head, and I am one of the chosen to debate against the extreme right-wing sects who want to blow up the Dome of the Rock, rebuild the Temple on its original site and reintroduce animal sacrifice!

I was overwhelmed with gratitude and in awe of the scholarship after reading Rabbi Cohen's report and looked forward to meeting him on Sunday morning.

The next meeting kicked off with the little rituals of the first meeting, but this time the Rabbi's demeanour was a little darker. He brushed aside my compliments and got straight to the point. "My dear friend, I too have been subjected to death threats but my route to this state of affairs is somewhat different to yours. We share a common purpose and I need your help.

The fraught matter of rebuilding the Temple and restoring the barbaric practice of animal sacrifice has resurfaced.

The Ashkenazi Chief Rabbi of Israel, David Lau, has recently made a speech saying he would like to see the Jewish temple rebuilt on the Temple Mount in Jerusalem. The Prime Minister has pledged to maintain the status quo that prohibits Jewish prayer at the site and has ordered members of the Knesset not to approach the Mount, a move contested by Jewish zealots bent to building the third temple. As the Charedi community is increasing in size and influence whilst secular Israelis are delaying and limiting their families, the population is divided on this issue. Yet it is not just a concern for Israeli domestic policy, the building of a Third Temple would destabilise the religious practices of the Jewish diaspora as well. The Israeli government recognises this and has allowed their rabbinical authorities to reconvene a Sanhedrin council of 71 sages representing all orthodox communities in the world. As chairman of the Rabbinic Council of the United Synagogues of Great Britain and the Commonwealth, I have been invited to attend. My position is simple, the status quo has served us well for 72 years and apart from relaxing the rules governing the right for Jews to pray on the Temple mount, confined to a limited area nowhere near the Dome of the Rock or the Al Aqsa Mosque, I'd rather things stayed that way.

From my sermons and publications, my opinions are well known, and I suspect the threats on my life come from the same source as yours. The Sanhedrin council was scheduled to meet just before *Pesach* last year but has been postponed for 12 months because of the pandemic.

It is now scheduled to take place in Jerusalem on the dates, March 20th-26th ending just before Shabbat and the first Seder night. The Zealots are hoping to celebrate the first night of the Passover on the Temple mount should they win a majority of votes from the council.

Apart from the threat to the cohesion of Judaism in the land of Israel and the diaspora, this would undoubtedly lead to another intifada. By fair means or foul and want to put an end to this idiocy and that is where you can help me."

"Yitzhak, I would do anything to help you win this debate, but I know nothing related to this problem."

"Robert, I'm not asking your help as a Talmud scholar, but as a molecular biologist."

"Now you've really captured my attention, go on give me a clue"

"I think you are too close to your subject to see what is obvious to me. Who should be making these decisions, the descendants of the conquered Kingdom of Judea, the Levites or the Cohanim?" I suddenly understood where he was coming from and couldn't suppress my laughter. "You cunning fox! Let me guess, there are more Cohanim on your side than on the other?" "Precisely! However, I am only going by their family names. Cohen, Coen, Khan and Katz for a start. Rappaport, Kaplan, Cowan and Kagan are other examples but not all those with the surname of Cohen are in fact Cohanim. For example, Cohen is a common Irish surname. A quick look at the list of the 71 of the select, suggests that our side has a greater proportion of Cohanim than the other side has a greater proportion of Levites. If you could somehow confirm my instinct, then I could conclude my remarks with a declamation, 'Who should have more authority in making this decision? The descendants of the High Priests of the first Temple or their servants?!'"

We both fell about with laughter, and I choked on my coffee. Once I'd regained control of myself, I realised the genius of the idea and began thinking of the practicalities.

"Brilliant idea Yitzhak now down to the practicalities. I could easily determine the presence of the Cohen module haplotype on the Y chromosome either by taking a sample from the oral mucosa or with a sample of their hair, but how could we approach these Rabbis whilst retaining confidentiality?"

"Don't worry Robert, I've already thought this through. We use the principle that the best place to hide a diamond is in a chandelier. You forget your celebrity status. With my endorsement as chairman of our Rabbinical Council and your status as a professor at UCL, you launch a new research programme trying to confirm your original findings on the prevalence of the Cohen modal haplotype on a large Jewish population, say 20,000, selected at random that 'by chance' include members of the Sanhedrin. This would need International collaboration but I'm sure your colleagues around the world would love to be co-authors of a paper that includes your name."

"Yes, that would work" I replied with enthusiasm, "But it would cost."

"Would a donation to your department from a wealthy benefactor of say £100,000 cover your costs?"

"Yes, that would do nicely, thank you. I shall now leave you and start writing the protocol for my new study".

We warmly embraced as I left the house having agreed to keep in close touch using code names for our e-mail exchanges. Our daughters' names at each exchange would stand for the project and Shabbat service would stand for the Sanhedrin meeting.

CHAPTER *16*

# LONDON DECEMBER 14ᵀᴴ, 2022

T HE morning broke with a crystalline egg-shell blue sky with a touch of frost on our lawn reflecting the light back looking like stars that had fallen during the night. I dressed in my best suit which was in fact a new navy-blue formal attire bought from the Marks & Spencer flagship store near Marble Arch. I had been dragged there reluctantly by my wife and daughter the previous week. Sophie and Chloe looked gorgeous in expensive looking outfits from somewhere much posher than M&S. We decided to take an Uber taxi rather than struggle to find a parking space near the British Museum. The event was scheduled to start at 12.30 and the printed programme looked like this.

**Nefertiti and the Exodus from Egypt**
**14/12/2022**
**A joint symposium by UCL and the British Museum**
**Stevenson Lecture Theatre**
**(Sponsored by the National Geographic)**

**Chairman Sir Arthur Penrose Provost UCL**

**12.30 Introductions by Dr Zahi Awass director of the department of antiquities Egypt**
**and Sir Bernard Fisher director of the British Museum.**
**13.00 The discovery of the three mummies at Saqqara—Professor Sharif Cairo University**

13.30 The Saqqara Codex—Professor Angus McCartney, Professor University of Leeds

14.00 The artefacts discovered with the mummies—Dr Ingrid Johansen Cairo University and Professor Lucy Carpenter University of Leeds.

14.30 Nefertiti's casket and the Golden death mask—Ingrid Johansen and Angus McCartney.

15.00 The crossing of the Reed Sea—Dr David Goddard
Tea

16.00 Stones, Bones and Genomes-A summing up—Professor Robert Abrahams, UCL

17.00 The formal opening of the exhibition at Sainsbury Exhibition Gallery

You may note that I got the best slot that was intentionally open-ended to allow questions.

We arrived about an hour early to allow me time to check the audio-visual system and left time for Sophie and Chloe to mingle with the great and the good waiting to be admitted. For security reasons seats in the auditorium, it was by invitation only, but all the proceedings were televised on the National Geographic channel.

The British Museum is a monstrosity that occupies a whole block at the corner of Gower Street and Great Russel Street. It was opened in the mid 19thC and at the time, was the largest building site in Europe. Its neo-classical frontage is grit-grey and foreboding but once you pass through the gigantic portico you enter into the Great Court which in contrast is a blaze of white light and is considered the most beautiful interior space in the country. This is all thanks to the genius of the architect Norman Foster who had the bright idea of covering the open courtyard with a roof of glass cut into triangles with the old reading room, a huge cylindrical edifice at the centre. The whole interior is painted white, and the reading room is encircled by a wide staircase to the upper floors of the museum.

Our foreign VIP visitors were awestruck on entering the world-famous museum but couldn't ignore the snake-like queue of the common folk and tourists waiting to view the exhibition even if it wasn't going to be officially opened for another four or five hours. In addition, the museum shop had its own queue and the effigies of Nefertiti's bust and framed facsimiles of the Saqqara codex were flying off the shelves. Clearly, our strategy had worked and if nothing else the day's events would be a financial success.

Once I was reunited with my wife and daughter, we returned to the magnificent auditorium and found our reserved seats in the second row. The first row had been reserved for our foreign VIP visitors as well as Princess Royal, the Chancellor of the University of London, and her entourage.

As chance would have it, Chloe found herself seated next to Ahmed the adopted son of David Goddard. This was his first visit anywhere outside Egypt. He had matured into a very handsome young man and by some wheeling a dealing I had found him a place at UCL's department of Egyptology to start in the new academic year in 2023. His expression was a delight to behold, he clearly thought that he had entered Nirvana, my beautiful teenage daughter on one side, Princess Anne in front and the magnificence of his surroundings. Chloe wore an expression of indifference although I was amused to catch her making sly glances weighing up her neighbour. Further along the row, I spotted Rabbi Cohen with his wife and daughter, invited as an acknowledgement of him securing funding for my department. I asked Chloe if she wanted to sit with the Cohen family, but she assured me she was perfectly happy with the view from where she was sitting.

The programme started on time and the chairman kept them to time. 25 minutes for the talk and 5 minutes for questions. All the speakers were very professional, and all the illustrations were engaging. The audience sat engrossed, but few had the courage to stand up to ask a question in the presence of Royalty. During the tea break, I introduced Sophie and Chloe to David's family. The wives immediately hit it off as if they had known each other forever whilst son and daughter avoided eye contact but despite his coffee-coloured skin, Ahmed's blush could not be hidden. By this time, I was getting a little agitated, not that I was nervous, I had a decade of experience lecturing to large audiences and as my talk and illustrations were well prepared there was no reason for concern. My agitation arose through an obsession with timekeeping. In the end, it was left to me to break up the tea party and persuade Sir Arthur and Princess Royal, with great respect, to get the show on the road again.

Princess Anne was charming and amused at my impertinence in shepherding them back into the Stevenson auditorium. My talk was well received and for simplicity's sake, I attach below an edited transcript that appeared in a special edition of the National Geographic a couple of months later.

## Stones, bones and genomes: The Exodus revisited

Your Royal Highness, Lords, Ladies and Gentlemen,

Before I launch into my talk, I need to start with a disclaimer. I have been accused of many things but one thing for sure I'm not an atheist although my concept of the almighty may not be identical to many in this audience. The problem emerges from the common belief of a binary distinction between those of the scientific community versus those of the Faith community. Focussing down on the context of my research you might think that there is a battle between Biblical historicity and what the Bible teaches us about moral philosophy. The late ex-Chief Rabbi, Lord Jonathan Sacks, put it beautifully in these words.

> Science will explain how but not why. It talks about what is, not what ought to be. Science is descriptive, not prescriptive; it can tell us about causes but it cannot tell us about purposes.

Furthermore, we should not lose sight of the fact that the history of the Children of Israel extends from about 4,000 BCE to the present day, whilst the span of time my colleagues and I have studied is in the region of 100 years between 1350 and 1250 BCE. You might think of it as a tiny sliver of time in the sandwich of bread slices each 3,000 years thick. Before planning this lecture, I sought the advice of my Rabbi, the Reverent Doctor Yitzhak Cohen who may not agree with everything I say yet at the same time even if true, it is no threat to Judaism or to the Abrahamic faiths.

The Biblical story of the Children of Israel in ancient Egypt starts with Joseph and ends with the Exodus. Rabbi Cohen provided me with the evidence that the Joseph of the Bible was in fact Imhotep the Vizier to the 3rd dynasty Pharaoh Djoser. He was the architect of the step pyramid at Saqqara, the very place where Professor Sharif discovered the three mummies of renown. Imhotep was made a prince of Egypt and just by looking at the names of the Pharaohs between the 3rd and 18th dynasties, you could make a case that the bloodline of Imhotep runs all the way through to Tuthmose, the hero of our story who wrote the words of wisdom and the code of moral philosophy on the Saqqara Codex described my colleague, professor Angus McCartney.

I started my involvement in this expedition in my role as a paleogeneticist. In other words, someone with his feet in both archaeology and molecular biology schools of thought.

My interest was provoked by two anomalies, first, the observation that the Cohen modal haplotype on the Y chromosome was found in over 70% of Jews all over the world who according to their oral evidence were Cohanim. We judged that this mutant variant was over 3,000 years old and first appeared in fewer than 30 antecedents. Yet the founders of this molecular marker could not have been Levites because those who claim this lineage have nothing in common in their genome. The other anomaly is that there are no data, no archaeological discoveries, and no skeletons, to support the story of a tribe with 800,000 warriors as described in Exodus, which would imply nearly 2M men, women, and children, migrating from Egypt to the Levant, in the years between 1,400–1,200 BCE.

Apologists for this negative observation claim that the tangible evidence was buried in the sands of time and yet we have solid proof from the archaeologic studies at Memphis, Thebes, Saqqara for the truth of the ancient Egyptian narrative as well as the wonderful bas reliefs from Nineveh in this venue that provides solid evidence for the narrative of the Assyrian Empire.

One bottom line on the Merpentan Stele in this museum claims to refer to the "victory over Israel", but that is very thin gruel in comparison with the remaining contents of the British Museum.

What our discoveries teach us for those with open minds, can be summed up as follows. The Pharaoh Akhenaten re-introduces monotheism and his wife, Nefertiti, becomes a devotee and a high priestess of the new cult. She has an affair with the court artist, Tuthmose, and has two sons with him, Imhotep and Tuthmose. Nefertiti dies of breast cancer, Tuthmose the creator of the famous Berlin portrayal, and their older son dies of a plague leaving their younger son, whom we like to claim is the Biblical Moses, to remain as the high priest of the monotheistic faith. After Nefertiti dies and with the succession of the boy King Tutankhamun, a counter-revolution occurs and the militia of all the other sects, gang up to destroy Amarna. This ends as they chase out the priests and their servants, who carry the mummy of Nefertiti with them for reburial at Saqqara, along with her partner and eldest son. The reburial of the Kings, Queens and Princes in ancient Egypt was common practice.

From there, the fugitives, in hot pursuit by a company of Egypt's finest cavalry, crossed the Canopic branch of the Nile Delta on dry land just in time before the deluge of the tsunami wave arrived to drown their enemy.

From there the priests, their families and their servants, numbering about 200, found their way to the traditional land of the sons of Jacob/Israel. The 40 years in the wilderness I would interpret as the time it took Moses to persuade the tribes to give up paganism and return to the monotheism of their forefathers, Abraham, Isaac and Jacob. The tribe of Dan remained intransigent and were driven out from the southwest of the future Kingdom to continue their pagan worship at the northernmost tip of what is now the new nation-state of Israel.

From about 1250 BCE, and Joshua's battle of Jericho, the Biblical narrative and the archaeological historicity run in parallel.

As far as the 10 plagues are concerned, I can't see how it matters whether you consider the miracles or acts of nature. As Baruch Spinoza once said.

**Deus sive Natura**

CHAPTER *17*

# Friday and Saturday at Yamin Moshe and the Old City of Jerusalem, Spring 2023

S OPHIE and Chloe elected to travel with me to enjoy the clement weather at this time of year in Jerusalem and make a vacation out of it with my expenses paid through department funds. Sophie had grown up in Israel, but Chloe had only visited once on the occasion of her Bat Mitzvah at the age of 1 2. At that time, we had a beach holiday staying at the Hilton in Tel Aviv. We wanted to take her to see the sights in Jerusalem, but she thought that was "boring" and preferred messing around in the pool overlooking the Mediterranean with her group of "Becks" from northwest London.

As always I enjoyed the view from the car window during the 40-minute drive up to Jerusalem from Ben Gurion airport to where we were to be accommodated in a guest house for distinguished guests of the Jerusalem Foundation called the almost unpronounceable, Mishkenot Sha,ananim. I had stayed there twice in the past, but Sophie and Chloe had no idea what to expect but were pleasantly surprised when our driver stopped just by the old stone-built Montefiore windmill. The driver helped us carry our luggage down some steep steps between pretty gardens and the golden glow of Jerusalem stone reflecting the late afternoon sun that shone brightly on my back.

We entered a modern foyer through smoked glass doors that enhanced the intrinsic beauty of an ancient stone-built hall. The driver left us, and we were immediately warmly welcomed by an attractive lady of middle years, who escorted us down another steep set of stairs as the complex was built into a cliff face.

Along the way to our rooms the walls were covered with photographs of the great and the good from the artistic and scientific disciplines from all over the world. Separating the doors to each apartment were little gardens of cacti and archaeological artifacts lit from above, all of which added to the charm of this delightful building. The nice lady showed us into our apartment and threw open the shutters that displayed a breathtaking view across the Kidron valley to the ancient Ottoman embattlements of the Old City.

That evening we had been invited to Friday night dinner at the home of my best friends in Israel who lived nearby at Yamin Moshe. Daniel Cohen was a professor of Archaeology at the Hebrew University and an expert on the period of the second Temple, his wife Jessie was a professor of molecular biology and shared similar interests to my own. We had even published papers together linked to the Biblical history concerning the distribution of the Ashkenazi mutation, BRCA1 amongst the Babylonian diaspora. Sophie had met them a number of times and on one occasion, embarrassed herself for suspecting I was having an affair with Jessie.

At 6.00 pm that evening, wearing our best smart casual outfits, the three of us walked up three levels of Jerusalem limestone steps to reach the windmill and then turned right which took us along a narrow footpath into the Yamin Moshe neighbourhood. Yamin Moshe is "the right hand of Moses" in Biblical Hebrew and this was the first housing project outside the walls of the Old City built in the early 19thC. The district consisted of four terraces of single-storey villas built into the hillside with stunning views, with each terrace separated from the one below with cascades of bougainvillaea, camellia, and azalea and hibiscus. These very desirable "cottages" were in fact built to house the artisans who would build west Jerusalem. Only the wealthy could afford them now, but very few of us knew that the Kettering prize money, the equivalent to the Nobel prize in the field of cancer research, paid for it thanks to Jessie Cohen's brilliant work on the Ashkenazi BRCA1 mutation.

House number 7 at level Aleph, sported a cobalt blue door, a colour that traditionally was thought to ward off the "evil eye" was doubly protected by a large mezuzah carved out of stone. The door was opened by Daniel Cohen, a tall, bronzed, handsome man wearing tortoise-shell glasses who showed us into a comfortable sitting room with a view facing the Old City. After the traditional hugs and kisses, glasses of wine were handed out and then Daniel turned at the sound of his wife entering from a back room. Daniel's wife insisted they called her by her nickname, Jessie, short for Yehudit- Esther. Jessie was tall and slim and walked like a gazelle. She had a preternatural beauty with emerald green eyes that seemed to be trans-illuminated. She was probably in her mid-40s, but it was difficult to judge. Again, there were warm embraces all around whilst Chloe appeared to be spellbound by Yehudit-Esther. Not long after that a very handsome young man, wearing a freshly ironed uniform of a captain in the IDF, bounded in from the kitchen and was introduced as the Cohen's son, Joseph-David, or Dave for short.

For Chloe it was love at first sight. Dave was entirely at ease in the company and made a beeline for Chloe and engaged her in conversation concerning the arts and theatre of famous *Old* London Town. The fact that *Old* London Town was built by the Romans about the same time the second Temple in Jerusalem was being knocked down by the same agents, wasn't given a second thought. I couldn't avoid eavesdropping on their conversation and was amused by this exchange. In desperation to make a good impression, Chloe chose to take an interest in the uniform of an IDF officer.

"Forgive me asking, but seeing the stars on your shoulder, should I call you Captain Cohen?"

"I am a captain, but you can call me Dave"

"OK Dave, why do you have a picture of a lion on your arm?"

"That's the Lion of Judah, the emblem of Central Command, amongst other areas we are meant to defend Jerusalem"

"OK, but what do the wings mean on your left chest and those pretty ribbons?"

"The wings also have a little parachute here and that means I'm in the parachute reserves and the ribbons tell you that I'm very brave in my conquests of beautiful young ladies who are teasing me."

At that, the pair of them burst out laughing as Chloe lost her cool and blushed from her neck to her ears. To me, it looked like a *shidduch* without the need for a matchmaker.

We then moved over to the dining area in the L shaped room where a table, covered in a brilliant white cloth, was set out for six. At one end of the table were twin candlesticks, a silver goblet and what looked like a table fountain with little spouts leading to six petite silver cups. The men covered their heads with small crocheted skull caps. Jessie lit the candles, covered her eyes with the palms of her hands and chanted a short blessing. Daniel then lifted up the goblet full of wine and in a beautiful baritone voice sang a blessing to welcome the Sabbath and bless the wine. He took a sip and poured the remainder into the mouth of the table fountain allowing the six cups to fill simultaneously. Each of those standing at the table was handed a silver cup and encouraged to sip the sacramental wine leaving the large cup that had been blessed by Daniel for Jessie to place next to the picture of her parents. Daniel then washed his hands with a jug and bowl on the sideboard and then lifted an embroidered linen cloth that was hiding two twisted choler loaves. He lifted the loaves and blessed the bread that was then torn into small pieces, salted and passed round to all his guests.

They then sat down to an exotic dinner of traditional Jerusalem Sephardic cuisine.

With the rituals out of the way and the first plates served, Daniel opened the conversation.

"Nuh Bobbala, what brings you to our golden city?"

Bobbala was the nickname my friends used when I was in Israel. It was a cross between Bob, the English abbreviation of my name and *boobala*, sweetheart in Yiddish. I chose to respond with half-truths.

"Well Danny boy, it's half term so that Chloe can come on holiday with us, Sophie wants to visit her parents in Mispe Ramon and I'm here to provide scientific advice for my friend Rabbi Dr Yitzchak Cohen, who is speaking as a member of the Sanhedrin on Sunday, *Erev Pesach*."

"Why does he need scientific evidence in this matter of faith?" responded Daniel.

"It's related to cruelty to animals and other details." I could see a twinkle of scepticism in his eyes, so I kept on talking.

"Anyway, what's your take on this nonsense of rebuilding the Temple?"

"Well Bobbala, you've spelt it out in the one sentence. Everyone in this room agrees it's nonsense but we only represent half of the population in Israel. We used to be a predominantly secular nation, but the Charedim have families averaging 9 whilst we, the secularists, have averaged 1.5 over the last 20 years. Bibi Netanyahu, always a populist, saw the writing on the wall and formed an alliance with the extreme right-wingers in the Knesset. He allowed the Charedi young men to escape military service, he buttered up the settler movement and did nothing to discourage the Temple builder fanatics. When he lost the last election to Naftali Bennet two years ago at the height of the third wave of the COVID-19 pandemic, the right-wingers thought it was now or never. They described this plague or pestilence as a warning from God and a punishment for our sins, and with both our chief rabbis on side, won the debate within our religious groups to convene a Sanhedrin to decide the matter. The last time the Sanhedrin met was 1,600 years ago. There have been several attempts to reconvene the Grand Sanhedrin in Israel since 1949 without success until today. The extremists won the day not just by evoking the wrath of Ha'Shem, but by calling on all the Charedi communities in the diaspora to have a voice as the rebuilding of the Temple would have an impact on the practice of Judaism, not just in Israel but all over the world. Although it was a cunning plan, they forgot the silent majority amongst the Conservative and Liberal Jewish communities in the USA, Europe and the Commonwealth. It now looks like it will be a close call rather than a slam dunk."

Captain Dave then joined in, "Professor Abrahams, there is another dimension to this that alarms me. Although these days as a reservist I only wear my uniform for one month in the year, I have a day-time job as well. I have a desk job at the department of the interior and I pick up vibes that are denied to the uninitiated. There is an extreme right-wing group or sect that is led by Rebbe Moishe ben Levy, they will not accept a vote that denies them a Temple and animal sacrifices and are covertly arming themselves and preparing for a civil war. We have them in our sights but just be careful about going outdoors on Monday. One way or the other there will be riots."

A cold chill came over me as I remembered how this sect attempted to destroy my reputation. I kept quiet so as not to alarm my family.

Jessie Cohen then interrupted the silence that followed her son's alert.

"That's enough doom and gloom, let's plan some sightseeing for our visitors. May I suggest that tomorrow morning we attend the early morning Shabbat service at our little synagogue next door and then we will take you all on a sight-seeing tour of the old City for Chloe's benefit. Then on Sunday, I will take Sophie and Chloe to the Israel Museum to see the Third Tablet of the Holy Covenant as well as their amazing collection of art."

"What's the Third Tablet of the Holy Covenant?" asked Chloe.

"All will be revealed on Sunday morning," replied Sophie enigmatically.

The next morning, we woke to a perfect blue cloudless sky and walked up-hill to Yamin Moshe and turned into the lowermost terrace to discover a very small Sephardi synagogue at 08.00 for a short service before setting out for the Old City.

We then walked down a long sequence of steps to the bottom of the Kidron Valley and then strode out across the Sultan's pool and up a winding path that lead directly to Zion gate at which point we entered the Armenian quarter of the Old City. Following the ancient Ottoman walls now on our right-hand side we soon entered the Jewish Quarter. Daniel then took us down some steep steps to the Roman Cardo, with the original paving stones leading precisely north-south. Here he pointed out the pillars and cubicles that marked out the main shopping centre of Jerusalem at the time of Jesus. Coming up for air again we took ourselves, via a network of narrow allies until we reached a beautiful courtyard facing due east known as the Al Buraq wailing wall plaza, where we enjoyed the breath-taking view of the Temple Mount and the golden-domed Islamic shrine, the Dome of the Rock. The rock inside was traditionally believed to be the site of the binding of Isaac where God stayed the hand of Abraham who was about to offer his son as a human sacrifice. The Muslims venerate this rock because they believed that it was from this point that the prophet Mohammed spurred on his mount Buraq and in one mighty leap entered heaven.

Leaving that viewpoint we made our way down another steep lane, passed through a security checkpoint and strolled across a huge plaza with the blazing sun burning the back of our necks, following a crowd of ultra-orthodox Jews wearing their traditional black suits and black hats in spite of temperatures now in the high 70's. Looking to our right it was obvious where this crowd were heading. There it was, the "Wailing Wall" or more correctly the Western Wall of the Temple Mount, standing 20 meters high and constructed out of huge limestone blocks. Packed two or three deep, were lines of nodding men facing the wall with their heads covered in prayer shawls. Young men in sun-bleached army fatigues, wearing crocheted skullcaps, punctuated these lines like a piano keyboard. As it was a Shabbat morning, several groups standing away from the wall were parading elaborately dressed scrolls of the Old Testament. In addition, young boys were reading from other scrolls on mobile lecterns because Shabbat was also the opportunity for the families of Bar Mitzvah boys to celebrate their coming of age. Chloe was surprised to hear women's voices ululating from behind a screen at the southern extremity of the wall. I encouraged her to walk down the plaza and join the women. When she got close, she witnessed a strange sight. Hundreds of women wearing a variety of exotic head coverings were crowded by the screen trying to get a good view of their son's or grandson's coming of age. Others who were praying to face the wall were inserting folded pieces of paper between the cracks. This she had already learnt from her guidebook, were hastily written prayers for good fortune or the healing of loved ones. On a whim, Chloe scribbled a note blessing her family and newfound friends. She then said a quick prayer and slid her note into a crevice alongside hundreds of others. She had no idea why she had been so impulsive but in truth, she was already suffering from the contagious disease known as the "Jerusalem Syndrome".

Already dehydrated we greedily sucked ice-cold water from our thermos flasks.

After a short rest, we were guided by Daniel up another set of steps at the far corner of the plaza, through another security barrier, under a series of deeply shadowed Roman arches and into the noisy souk of the Christian quarter.

As we climbed the covered alleyway, our feet had to negotiate a flight of narrow steps, hollowed out and polished by the thousands of pilgrims who had passed this way over two millennia. The steps were split into three cascades by parallel concrete strips that provided a tramline for the constant and hazardous wheeled handcarts carrying produce and merchant's wares supplying the little boutiques that ran the full length of the souk as far as the eye could see. Exotic colors, exotic smells and exotic vendors on all sides assailed our senses as we made our way cautiously along the narrow thoroughfare. I was an old hand at the game and told my daughter to ignore the merchants. Chloe, however, was an innocent abroad and her natural English way of conducting herself, slowed them down as she very politely declined the offers of crucifixes, rosaries, heavily encrusted orthodox religious icons and authenticated wood fragments from the true cross. Instead of her polite rebuttals silencing the clamor of the vendors it appeared to inflame their generosity of spirit to the nice pretty English girl with offers of, 40%, 50%, OK just for you madam special price 60% discount! In the end, Daniel had to intervene with a rapid exchange of Arabic to put an end to the harassment of his charges. We then heard the sound of gospel song from further up the slope where a group of colourfully dressed African pilgrims had rested their feet by the VIth station of the Via Dolorosa, known as the Veil of Veronica. We continued our slow ascent until station IX where the signs pointed off to the right in the direction of the Church of the Holy Sepulcher. The final stations leading to the entombment of Jesus were to be played out in the church itself. The church, said to be the epicentre of the Christian faith, was blacked with soot and looked thoroughly unkempt. This was because of the constant squabbling amongst the Catholic, Greek Orthodox and Armenian Church custodians constantly inhibited the up-keep of this Holy site. There was so little commonality of purpose amongst these three branches of the Christian faith that the doorway and keys to the door of the Holy Sepulcher were by tradition, entrusted to two Muslim families.

On entering the Church there was a scene of bedlam. Four separate services seemed to be going on at the same time in churches within churches and side chapels within side chapels. Multiple groups of pilgrims attended by the priests of their particular denomination in their own peculiar garb and headgear were either kneeling in prayer or walking in awe at the last few stations of the cross.

Everywhere was incense, gold and bejewelled icons of Mary and Jesus, Jesus on the cross, Jesus being laid to rest and Jesus' resurrection. The heat and smell were insufferable, and the noise was like something from the Tower of Babel. Chloe started climbing a narrow set of steps clutching a brass handrail that ran around a huge misshapen rock that was said to be Golgotha, the place of the crucifixion of Jesus. She then came over faint and would have fallen all the way down if it wasn't for the kindly attention of a group of Irish nuns who caught her as she stumbled and with my help, propelled her through the crush to a stone bench in the plaza outside.

This was clearly enough for one day, so we took the shortcut to come up for air at the Damascus gate and took taxis for the short ride back to the Montefiore windmill for a welcome siesta.

# CHAPTER 18

# THE GREAT DEBATE
# JERUSALEM SUNDAY, MARCH 21ST, 2023

THE obvious venue for the great debate was the Belz Chasidic great synagogue, the largest in Israel. It had room for 7,000 congregants and sufficient cushioned armchairs in an open rectangle close to the Ark for the 71 members of the Sanhedrin, chosen from the greatest scholars from around the world, according to the numbers in the community they represented. The British and Commonwealth orthodox community is relatively small and worthy of only two representatives, the Chief Rabbi and my friend Rabbi Doctor Yitzhak Cohen. The meeting was to be chaired jointly by the Ashkenazi and Sephardi Chief Rabbis in Israel. They sat in highchairs on either side of the Ark. I sat near the back and could barely see the platform for the speakers but fortunately, the audio system worked well and there were large free-standing flat-screen monitors all down the isles so that the audience could also enjoy the view. I found it ironic that we should be debating a return to the "Iron age" using the technology of the "Space-age".

The proceedings started with the morning service, *shakrit*, repeated twice to satisfy the two different traditions represented by the two Chief Rabbis chairing the meeting.

The plan was to control the debate according to the Oxford Union rules. In other words, we would vote on the motion, "Does this house agree to rebuild the Temple on the Temple Mount and restore animal sacrifice as commanded by the Torah?"

There were to be 8 speakers, representing those for and against the motion from Israel and those for and against the motion from the diaspora. Of these two were chosen from the USA and the others represented two from Europe. To my surprise, three of those arguing against the motion wore the garbs of orthodox communities, yet negating my prejudices, all argued as rational and humane logisticians. They all quoted Maimonides and I was proud to hear the names of two British ex-chief Rabbis, Lord Jakobovits and Lord Sacks, mentioned to make their case.

A vote would be taken at the start and then the proposers and seconders from each side would speak for 20 minutes, there would then be questions from the floor for 40 minutes.

The proposers for and against the motions would summarise their arguments in 5 minutes each before a final vote was taken. I was amused to think that this mode of debate had been invented at Oxford University in the days of King Henry the VIIIth and was now being used to settle a controversy going back to King Herod the Great. Even to agree the wording of the motion took an hour of argument but the speakers had been chosen in advance. I was delighted to learn that my Rabbi had been chosen to lead the argument against the motion representing European Jewish communities. He had kept this as a close secret all along. Leading the argument for the motion was my nemesis, Reb Moishe ben Levy, the leader of the Sabbatai Zevi sect.

The debate was to be vocalised in Biblical and Talmudic Hebrew with subtitles on the screen in modern Hebrew and English.

Before the motion was proposed a vote of the 71 members of the Sanhedrin was taken.

It was a close call, with 33 voting for the motion, 34 voting against the motion and 4 abstaining.

Reb Moishe Ben Levy kicked off, and the content of his rant could be summarised by the words of William Shakespeare in Macbeth's famous soliloquy, "It was full of sound and fury signifying nothing". All I could make out from the translation was that God commanded it through the voice of Moses and God had sent the pestilence as the first warning. If we disobeyed God at this time it would be the end of the world, another flood or a mighty earthquake. I was astounded that anyone in their right mind would believe this bullshit! Yet still he ran out of time and the speaker had to be manhandled away from the lectern by ushers.

Then it was Yitzhak Cohen's turn. He spoke in a modest and measured way that captivated the audience and for the first time, I came to appreciate the charisma of this modest man and why he had been chosen. These words were included in his peroration.

> Now let me turn to the barbaric custom of sacrificing animals on the altar. This is more than medievalism; it is taking us back to the bronze age. The Talmud, the oral law that was debated by greater sages than us in the 3rd to the 6thcenturies of the Common Era came up with the code of conduct known as Tza'ar ba'alei chayim ( סייח ילעב רעצ), literally "suffering of living creatures", is a Jewish commandment which bans causing animals unnecessary suffering. This concept is not clearly enunciated in the written Torah, but was accepted by the Talmud as being a biblical mandate.
>
> We are not talking about the humane method of slaughter of shechita for feeding the hungry, we are talking about dragging a screaming bullock onto an altar in order to seek favour from God. What kind of God is that?! A God who can be persuaded to save us from an apocalypse via the stench of burnt flesh? He is no God of mine and no God of the Children of the new State of Israel gathered here today.

He sat down to thunderous applause from most of the audience, but they had no vote, and I couldn't see the expressions on the faces of the 70 members of the Sanhedrin when my friend sat down.

The other speakers supporting the motion said nothing original or captivating, droning on and on quoting Talmudic references. One of the American speakers against the motion, I learnt, was medically qualified and worked as a paediatrician and ethicist at Mount Sinai Hospital in New York. This seemed quite appropriate. The questioning from the other members of the conclave was overall, ill-tempered, and again balanced between for and against. It didn't light again up until it was the turn of Rabbi Isaac Cohen, to sum up his arguments against the motion. I almost remember that word for word.

"Chief Rabbis, my honourable rabbinical friends, Ladies and Gentlemen, I am but a humble Rabbi from Northwest London, but I have the advantage of living in the 21st century of the common era and look to the future of a thriving Jewish community all around the world. I'm inclusive and welcome all kinds of Jews of every hue and of every extreme of religiosity and for that matter even those Jews who claim they have no religion at all. Those who would vote in favour of the motion only look back to a primitive time in human development and refuse to engage with modern thinking. They are the ones who will destroy Am Yisrael and yet they are the biggest hypocrites. They deny scientific advances yet are happy to spread their message via the props of modernism, including the audio-visual aids of today's debate. They drive Volvos yet deny the internal combustion engine, they fly from Crown Heights in NYC, yet deny jet propulsion, they accept the latest innovations in medical care yet believe that their God heals them by the power of prayer. They accept the miracles of molecular biology when it comes to choosing a wife for their sons to avoid them marrying a girl with a genetically inherited disease. Well, I would like to help them make their decision with the latest study on the genetic inheritance that is relevant to all of us on this platform. My dear friend and colleague, Prof Robert Abrahamson, has just completed the latest study on the inheritance of the Cohen modal haplotype on the Y chromosome. Amongst those on the panel he was able to voluntary test the majority of those present as part of a study involving 20,000 Jews all over the world who claimed by oral tradition were either Cohanim or Levites. It turns out that most of us who are against this motion test positive for this mutation, whilst the majority of those who are for the motion have no specific genetic markers at all. So, my dear Chief Rabbis, dear colleagues, ladies and gentlemen, should this important decision be made by the direct descendants of the High Priest, Aaron, or by the servants of the priesthood, the Levites?!"

He sat down with a sphinx-like smile as pandemonium broke out amongst all those present. Most of the noise came from the hurrahs but there were some notable profanities from the fundamentalist group on the platform. It took several minutes before the Chief Rabbis' call for order was established at which point Reb Moshe ben Levy was called to the lectern.

He stood up tall, black in dress, black in beard and black in the expression on his face, before screaming out a curse, a *herem* and an ex-communication directed at me.

*"By decree of the angels and by the command of the holy men, we ex-communicate, expel, curse and damn Professor Robert Abrahams, with the consent of God, blessed be He, and with the consent of the entire holy congregation, and in front of these holy scrolls with the 613 precepts which are written therein: cursing him with ex-communication. Cursed be he by day and cursed be he by night; cursed be he when he lies down and cursed be he when he rises up. Cursed be he when he goes out and cursed be he when he comes in. And for his sins for which we incur the penalty of lashing for rebelliousness.*

*And for his sins for which we incur the penalty of forty lashes. And for his sins for which we incur the penalty of death by the hand of Heaven. And for his sins for which we incur the penalty of excision and childlessness. And for his sins for which he incurs the penalty of the four forms of capital punishment executed by the Court: stoning, burning, decapitation and strangulation. "*

At his command about 30 of the members of the Sanhedrin, stood up and walked out without waiting for the second ballot that would certainly have gone against them at this time.

CHAPTER *19*

# THE OCCUPATION OF TEMPLE MOUNT

T HE Israel Museum is built up of a chain of glass cubes linked in a knight's move pattern. The whole complex had been reopened in 2011 after extensive refurbishment and was in pristine condition reflecting the late morning sun of the Judean hills off every surface. To reach the sloping underground entrance to the museum one had to pass through beautifully landscaped gardens with spectacular views over the seven hills of Jerusalem and each viewpoint is occupied with a piece of contemporary sculpture from the world's most famous sculptors. Blissfully unaware of the events taking place in the Great Synagogue, Sophie and Chloe, led by Jessie Cohen, entered the museum. Chloe, who was studying the history of art for her A level exams at the end of the next term, wanted to visit the famed collection of impressionist and post-impressionist paintings. In order to reach those galleries, they first had to pass through a sequence of small synagogues that had been rescued from Eastern Europe at the end of the second world war and faithfully reconstructed in the Israel museum. Along the way they passed vitrines full of mediaeval Judaica that Chloe found boring. The spectacular collection of art works was everything the teenage girl valued and the sunburst of colour on entering the white walled galleries, took her breath away. Jessie then explained the tragic story behind this collection. Most of the paintings on view were works looted by the Nazis at the time of the Holocaust and their original owners were then murdered in the death camps. During the war a group of allied soldiers, expert in fine art, who called themselves the Monument Men, recovered thousands of priceless works many of which found their way to the Israel museum as the families who built up the collections no longer existed.

They spent an hour admiring the art during which time Chloe was dictating revision notes into her smart phone to help revise for the exams.

After a coffee break, Jessie guided them to the galleries displaying the collection of Biblical artefacts dating back to the battle of Jericho. She zoned in on a cuboidal vitrine bearing a rectangular stone that had been split down the center, uplighted in a violet hue and as far as Chloe could see, bore no marked features. Jessie then turned to her companions and in a theatrical tone of voice embarked on a well-rehearsed tutorial.

"Tell me Chloe, how many tablets of stone did Moses offer the Children of Israel?"

"That's easy, two" she replied.

"Wrong, there were 5! Let me now explain. The two tablets of the holy covenant bearing the 10 mosaic laws are those with which we are familiar and of course, they have never been discovered after the Romans carried away the Ark of the covenant at the fall of the second temple. However, if you read the Bible correctly there were two other tablets that Moses inscribed, that were initially rejected by the children of Israel and in a temper tantrum, he smashed the tablets on the ground. Tradition has it that all fragments of the holy law, or for that matter all pages from the holy books, must be buried with respect. It is believed that the first tablets of stone that were broken by Moses, were within the Ark of the holy covenant together with the second version of the decalogue. Very few people are aware of the third tablet of the holy covenant which you see before you."

By this time Jessie had collected a small group of young soldiers from the IDF, who seemed to be captivated by the sight of two beautiful women and one very pretty teenager listening to a scholarly talk about a blank chunk of rock.

Jessie then pulled out a small notebook from her shoulder bag before continuing.

"Let me now read to you a passage from Deuteronomy 27 verses 1–12.

*Moses and the elders of Israel commanded the people saying, observe the entire commandment that I command you this day. It shall be on the day that you crossed the Jordan to the land that has Hashem, your God gives you, you shall set up a stone and build an altar for Hashem, your God, an altar of stones you shall not raise iron upon them. You shall inscribe on it all the words of the Torah when you crossover you shall erect this stone on Mount Ebal, and you shall coat it in plaster and you shall inscribe on the stone all the words of this Torah well clarified. Take this tablet of the Torah and place it at the side of the Ark of the covenant of Hashem and it should be there for you as a witness.*

My father, Professor Martin Tanner, discovered this tablet of stone, fractured in two halves, embedded in the walls of an ancient synagogue at the Lebanese border. It bears an invisible copy of a summary of the 10 commandments than only showed up by scanning it for particles of iron from the tools that made the inscription. It looks like nothing much but is probably the most important artefact in the museum."

She stopped to catch her breath and was rewarded with a slow hand-clap from the 6 young soldiers that had now surrounded them. At first, Jessie thought this was very rude and then she suddenly realised that their behaviour was sinister. Before she could shout out a warning, all three of them were blinded by sacks pulled over their heads. They had no chance of fighting their wait out of the clutches of two young strong men who dragged them to the floor tying the neck of the sack around their ankles.

In the meantime, a renegade unit of the IDF had cordoned off the museum and were waiting for the three hostages to be dumped in a truck that speeded off in the direction of the Old City.

After the calamitous climax of the debate, I made my way out to meet up with Yitzchak Cohen in the courtyard of the Belz synagogue. We had agreed on a meeting point in advance that was just as well as there were TV vans and reporters all over the place many of whom were looking for the notorious Professor Abrahams. Fortunately, very few people in Israel knew what I looked like. Having linked up with my partner in crime and to avoid death by stoning, we jumped into a waiting taxi and took off to my lodgings by the windmill. We had invited Daniel and Jessie Cohen to join us for a post-mortem on the day's event. We reached Yamin Moishe about 20 minutes later and walked down the steps to my apartment. Sophie and Chloe weren't back yet from their visit to the Museum, so we sat outside on the terrace looking at the iconic view of David's Tower and the Armenian Basilica. About an hour later there was a knock at the door that I assumed would be Daniel and Jessie, but only Daniel was there looking agitated. He rushed inside and without another word turned on the TV. A view of the Dome of the Rock appeared in the background and speaking into an array of microphones was Reb Moishe ben Levy. He was speaking in Ivrit with English subtitles. Daniel translated as the leader of the Shabtai Zvi sect held forth. Apparently, a corps of soldiers who were of the extreme right-wing religious factions had shaved off their beards and *payot*, and with a well-planned attack, raided the Temple mount, murdering any Muslims that got in their way, and taking control of the plateau having blasted their way through the main access to the mount, a covered ramp that ran from the edge of the western wall plaza to the top of the western wall. They had placed explosives around the circumference of the interior of the Dome of the Rock and had taken hostages that were imprisoned inside the sanctuary. To my horror, he then showed a video clip of Sophie, Chloe and Jessie with hands tied behind their backs and their mouths covered by adhesive tape. His demand was clear and simple. Unless his followers were permitted to build the third Temple alongside the Dome of the Rock, they would kill their hostages and destroy the sanctuary. That was his last recourse even though he knew it would lead to a war between Israel and her Islamic neighbours. This would be the sign of Hashem to initiate Armageddon after which the Messiah will proclaim a new beginning. Until the foundations of the new Temple were built, they would keep the three hostages who would be treated well in their prison for as long as it takes. The picture on the TV then changed to a view of the Temple mount from a drone that showed about 200 soldiers carrying assault rifles forming a ring around the borders of the plateau. The camera then zoned in on ben Levy who concluded.

"The choice is yours, the Temple or Armageddon. You have 48 hours to decide!"

And then the screen went blank. After a few moments "normal" service was resumed, by that I mean a babble of news anchor-men and anchor-women passing opinions, interpreting the options, and interviewing any member of the Knesset they could drag off the streets. Daniel turned off the TV with a look of disgust on his face.

He turned to face me with tears rolling down his cheeks but before he could say the first words his mobile phone buzzed. He put the phone to his ear and listened intently for a few minutes and closed the conversation with six words, "Yes Sir, I'm on my way".

As he made for the door, he turned to face me and Rabbi Cohen to say, "The Prime Minister has requested my presence. I will try and keep in touch by text message whenever possible. Rabbi Cohen now is the time to pray for salvation to your God, a God of compassion, not the God of ben Levy, who demands animal and human sacrifice."

CHAPTER *20*

# THE PRIME MINISTER'S COMMAND CENTRE

T HE Prime Minister's command centre is deep below the ministry of defence not far from the building known as the Knesset, or House of Parliament. As Daniel Cohen is let in after a cascade of security measures, he is at first blinded by the darkroom illuminated by banks of video images showing all sections of the Temple mount from the sides and views from above from a swarm of miniature drones. Apart from the video images, there is a simple map of the plateau. The Prime Minister, Naftali Bennet, served as an officer of the *Maglan* commando unit during the Lebanese war in the 1990s and behind the smooth veneer of a successful businessman, for one month each year, he returned to serve in his regiment. As such he was qualified to lead the assault on Temple mount. He waves Daniel over to sit next to him at the head of a rectangular table facing the display of images. He then introduces him to the others sitting down with him. There is the deputy Minister of Defence, the new Chief of the General staff of the IDF, the chief of the Israeli Airforce, IAF, and the general commanding Central Command. There are the heads of Shin Bet and Mossad (equivalent to MI5 and MI6) and to his surprise, there is also the new head of the Palestinian West Bank Authority, Marwan Ben Sadat, who replaced President Mahmoud Abbas only a few months ago. Then with a mischievous smile the Prime Minister introduced him to the young officer at his right hand. As might be expected it was his son Captain David Cohen. Daniel heart fell into his stomach and he broke out into a cold sweat when he realised that his son would have to lead the parachute reserves in any attempt to secure the Temple Mount. "Professor Cohen it was your son's idea that we consult you at this time and you'll soon understand why when you look at the map in front of you. This is a simplified map of our battle zone. You will note the position of Dome of the Rock. Superimposed on this is an outline of your own estimate of the original position of King Herod's Temple shown in blue. Our enemies are expecting us to attack from their flanks and via helicopters above but the last place they would expect an assault would be from within the Dome itself. Captain Cohen tells me that you may know a secret route that might take us to the interior of the Holy shrine of our Islamic friends. Our new brother in arms who has common purpose with us, President Marwan Ben Sadat, would endorse this manoeuvre if this was the only way of saving the Dome of the Rock and Avoiding Armageddon. Please tell us what you think. We will provide a WIFI link to your files if required.

Daniel responded with veracity as if he had already considered this option.

"Yes, this is the case and to this day some of what you are about to hear has been covered by the government's secrecy laws. It is a long story, but I'll keep it short.

On August the 11th, 1960, which coincided with the 9th of Av 5720, there was a major earthquake that even cracked the walls of the Knesset. The epicentre of the quake was in the North not far from Safad and amongst other damage the foundations at one corner of the ancient synagogue in Peki'in. It stands to this day but can trace its history back to 73 CE. The daughter of the family who were custodians of the shul, whose name was Sara Zenati, who happened to be the mother of my mother-in-law, discovered a cedar wood box bearing four scrolls that dated to the time of the fall of the second Temple.

These scrolls told the story of the twin daughters of the deputy High Priest, who managed to escape the conflagration that destroyed the Temple. They joined the Zealots at Masada and then in 73 CE escaped the mass suicides. One of the sisters made it to the northern reaches of the old Kingdom of Israel and founded the Zenati synagogue where the scrolls were discovered. One of these scrolls describes how, with the help of their dying father, they escaped from the interior of the Temple and found their way out to safety. That scroll is named Codex Yehudit II and I'll now search for it on my laptop and if you can allow to share my screen on one of your monitors you can read the translation from the paleo-Hebrew yourselves."

It only took Daniel 5 minutes to download the file in question and then beam it to all the assembly.

*Chapter 21*

# THE CODEX YEHUDIT II, JERUSALEM 9ᵀᴴ AV 3791 (70 CE)

*Blessed art thou, O Lord our God; endow my daughters with the spirit of Sarah, Rebecca, Rachel, and Leah. May the Lord bless thee and keep thee: may the Lord make his face to shine upon thee: may the Lord turn his face unto thee and give thee peace.*

WITH that, he reached out and with all the strength left to him pulled down hard on the golden rope that drew the curtains that protected us from the force of the divine presence at the epicentre of our faith. *The curtains parted and Eliezer Ha'Cohen, blessed of the Almighty, departed this life. His two guards laid him down, covered his body with a white sheet of linen ripped from the nearest wall of the court and, carefully avoiding a glance into the Holy of Holies, bowed stiffly to us, grunted a muted blessing of their own, unsheathed their swords, and rushed out to guard the portals to the gates of the Court of Israel. As the curtains parted, we expected to be blinded by a flash of brilliant white light, the divine presence of the Almighty. As it was, it took our eyes a few moments to adjust to the dim light reflected from the walls of white linen lining the sides and roof from the diffused ruby glow of the everlasting light. As our eyes adjusted and we saw what was in front of us, we threw ourselves to the floor and lay flat on our faces with our arms outstretched, afraid to look at the face of the Lord. But nothing happened and* the expected roar of disapproval never materialized; the only sound to leak into this holy space was the muted roar from the battle being fought outside the Temple Mount.

After a minute or two my curiosity got the better of me and I tilted my head and squinted through my right eye. The face I had imagined was a trick of the light reflected back from the central object in this Holy of Holies; surely this was the Ark of the Covenant, the Aron Kadesh; the light of the world. The Ark was about two and a half cubits in length, a cubit and a half wide and the same in height. It was covered in gold and around each edge of the rim was a crown of great complexity whose details I could not make out. But the most startling aspect of this divine object was the pair of cherubim rising from its top surface. The one on my right had the face of a female child and the one on my left the face of a male child. They appeared to be crafted from solid gold. Each carried the wings of a bird that arched over the Ark and touched in the centre as if to protect the tablets within. We had first met these angels woven into the curtains closing the entrance to the sanctuary and we saw them again worked into the ceiling of the tent. From the side of the Ark facing me I saw two gold rings the size of my wrist, and through these rings ran two long staves covered in gold. These I had learned were used for carrying the Ark during the wanderings in the desert over a thousand years ago in our long history. The weight of the acacia wood of the construction and the weight of gold in its ornamentation must have crushed those who attempted to carry it on their shoulders, yet legend had it that the Ark of the Covenant carried its bearers rather than the other way around. The staves were permanently left in place, we had been taught, to symbolize that the word of the Lord would always follow his chosen people in their wanderings rather than remain fixed forever in their resting place upon the rock where Abraham had been ordered to offer his son, Isaac, in sacrifice.

We could have lain there in awe and rapt attention were it not for the muted screams getting closer to the perimeter walls of the sanctuary, suggesting that one of the outer walls of the temple complex had been breached. As one we shot upright and turned to each other. What now? At that point I remembered the scrolls clutched in my sweaty fists that contained our father's instructions. Backing in respect a few paces from the Ark, we started to read in unison by the light of the everlasting light. In father's neat Hebrew script, in red ink upon ochre-coloured vellum, a sequence of directives appeared as we unrolled the scrolls from their central wooden spindle.

*Scroll this far and no further; fulfil my commandments lest you die. Eat of the showbread sprinkled with frankincense to build your bodily and spiritual strength.*

As we were starving, this was a command we hastened to obey. We turned toward the sacred table and each grabbed a fresh loaf of the show-bread that would never again be used in the Sabbath ritual, took a pinch of frankincense from the silver spoon on the top shelf and ate with relish. Whether it was our starvation or not, I'll never know, but this bread was the tastiest I've ever enjoyed, with a uniform crust that melted in the mouth. It tasted as if it had been baked with honey as on the feast of the New Year. Only in retrospect did I wonder by what miracle the fresh loaves of bread awaited us. When we had eaten our fill, I felt restored and strangely at peace with myself, even though I was mourning for our beloved father. Nodding to each other we turned the scroll carefully until the next commandment appeared and at its sight the spindle fell from my hands in shock and disbelief. We were commanded to desecrate the Ark of the Covenant! Was our father mad? He had commanded us to break into the Holy Ark and extract the third tablet! And that was not all: we were commanded to break it in two. Esther and I conferred for a short while and agreed there was no going back. The choice was stark; retreat and end up raped and murdered by the mob or follow the fifth commandment to honor thy father and thy mother—but at the same time risk the wrath of God. The choice was made for us as we heard the crash of timber signaling the destruction of the great doors guarding the entry to the first of the temple's courts. Repeating the Shema, "Hear, O Israel, the Lord thy God the Lord is one," we approached and placed our hands on the cherubim, one at each end. Praying that the lid was not fastened to the body of the Ark, we braced ourselves to lift the heavy golden shield comprising the roof, the golden crown, and the conjoined cherubim that covered and protected the tablets brought down by Moses from the mountain. To our astonishment, the lid and its superstructure lifted effortlessly, suggesting either that we had ac-quired superhuman strength by eating the showbread or that, as in the legend; the Ark carried its bearers.

We laid the lid of the Ark on the floor with reverent care and peered into the dark interior. At once an aroma of old timber and spice wafted up to our noses and as one, we responded with a hearty sneeze. I could have sworn I heard the traditional response of 'labriut'—bless you—come from above but the rational part of my brain suggested it was an echo. Inside the box was another golden box whose elaborate lid, crafted in gold with bas-relief figures, *appeared to illustrate the sun disc whose rays shone a figure dressed as an Egyptian prince.*

*The lid to the inner box also yielded easily to our combined effort and inside that was yet a third box of ancient cedar wood without decoration that smelt of frankincense and myrrh. The lid of the third box, made of a sturdy wooden panel the thickness of my thumb and still a perfect rectangle after more than a thousand years, gave way to our efforts almost as if there were a hand pushing from below as we lifted from above. A cloud of the dust of ages followed the lid as we placed it next to its fellows on the floor of the sanctuary and we steeled ourselves once more to peer within the ultimate box holding the tablets of stone inscribed by Moses our patriarch, brought down from Mount Sinai, inscribed with God's laws to instruct the tribes of Israel.*

*By now we were trembling in terror. Once again reciting the Shema, we prepared ourselves to look upon the holiest relic in the history of the world. As predicted by our father, there were three rough-hewn slabs of stone. Two were of similar size, rectangular in shape, measuring about one and a half arm's length and half that in width. The third, lying on top of the other two, was a smaller rectangle, measuring about ten hand's spans on the long side and six hand's spans on the short side. We paused again, terrified of laying hands on the words of the Almighty as taken down in chisel strokes by the hand of Moses. Egged on by the increasing clamor from without the walls of the sanctuary, we bent down and with some difficulty, this time, lifted out the smaller stone.*

*Its unexpected weight caused us to drop it on the outer edge of the Ark, and with a crack that sounded like thunder, the tablet split perfectly in two, making two rectangles. By this time, we had run the full gamut of emotions from terror to awe to simple surprise, and we fell to our knees to inspect the two fragments of the third tablet of stone. The deeply cut letters appeared in ten symmetrical lines divided through the center. They were written in some ancient form of the alphabet that we couldn't decipher. Without another thought, we returned the three lids to their appropriate places and completed the reading of our father's last testament. With an economy of words, our directives were made clear.*

*Take this stone tablet and wrap it in hangings from the walls of the sanctuary.*

*From this point on, each of you will be custodians of these holy relics carrying the tablet to a sanctuary in the north. Find the passage of King Herod beneath the flagstone that bears the Ark of the Covenant. The scarab will be* your guide. At the bottom of that shaft you will find men's clothing. Replace your linen robes and dress in the manner of a man. King Herod's passage runs from the Antonia fortress to the north— do not turn that way: follow the tunnel under the temple to the south until it reaches its junction with King Hezekiah's tunnel that runs at a deeper level. Follow it 1,200 cubits farther south until it emerges outside the walls of the lower city at the Gihon spring in the Valley of Kidron. There you will be met by two of my most trusted friends. Do not be surprised by their appearance and when they ask you "Are you the sons of Eliezer Ha'Cohen?" answer yes and from then on carry out their instructions as if they were from your father who now sojourns in Gan Eden. May God shine his face upon you and be gracious unto you. Amen

### Eliezer ben Yakov ha'Cohen

Without pausing for thought we began to carry out our instructions. As an added sacrilege we tore down the curtains covering the front of the sanctuary and tore them into strips. These strips of precious fabric were used to parcel the stone fragments and golden candlesticks. We bound them up with the braided gold ropes that had made up the curtain pulls. We then turned our attention to the Ark. Esther and I grabbed a pair of handles and each of the ends of the staves passing through the loops at the sides of Aron Kadesh and braced ourselves to lift the heavy object made up of three boxes of cedar and acacia wood, two of which were covered in gold and the outermost one capped with the golden cherubim. In retrospect we estimated that their combined weight must have been at least five talents. We were surprised again at the ease with which we were able to lift it and put it to one side. Where the Ark had stood were paving stones of white, glistening marble, in all likelihood seeing the light of day for the first time since King Herod and his priests con-secrated the temple. There were four perfectly cut and closely fitting flagstones and at their central junction one contained a carefully sculptured bas-relief image of a scarab measuring a finger's length. The symbolism of this was not lost on us. The scarab, or dung beetle, was worshipped by the Egyptians as the embodiment of the god Khepri, the god of the rising sun who was credited with rolling the sun to the horizon each morning as the scarab rolled its ball of dung to its nest. The crushing of this image under the weight of the Ark surely symbolized the victory of the one God over the pantheon of deities of the pagan faith of the pharaohs.

Gingerly I pressed the palm of my hand on the pagan image, but nothing happened. It was only when the scarab felt the full weight of my body that the *flagstone started to tilt on an axis diagonally from corner to corner. Esther grabbed me before I stumbled and we watched in disbelief as the stone turned silently on hidden hinges until it rested in perfect balance vertically, leaving two triangular holes just sufficiently large to allow us entry into the tunnel below.*

*We looked down into the dark space and realized we would need a source of light in order to continue our mission. There was only one source of flame available to us and that was the everlasting light; and to rob the everlasting light to show us the way seemed for once strangely appropriate. Once again, we tore strips off the wall hangings and fashioned them into two crude torches making a hand grip by binding them around with the remnants of the curtain pull. We carried the showbread table to a point below the light and Esther clambered up while I held out the first of the torches that quickly caught fire from the flame within the ruby bowl.*

*Our torches illuminated the tunnel below the tilted scarab stone. There was a short drop of about three cubits, with iron hoops on the wall to act as footholds. At the base of the shaft we saw two bundles wrapped in sheepskin and also two oil lamps with carrying handles. Clearly our father had not left us entirely to our own devices.*

*I threw my legs over the gaping triangular hole and carefully let myself down while Esther held the two torches. Once my feet touched the ground, I picked up one of the oil lamps, climbed halfway back, and lighted the lamp from Esther's torch. I climbed back down and lit the second lamp—and then I heard Esther scream.*

*As the doors of the Court of Israel came crashing open under the on-slaught of the Roman battering rams, Esther had dropped one of the torches, which had ignited the remnants of the bone-dry curtains, and in no time at all the four walls and tented ceiling were ablaze. Quickly Esther dropped through the hole. Halfway down she tilted the stone back into place on its marvelously crafted spindle. The gap above our heads sealed itself with a hiss, protecting us from the conflagration we had left behind and the Roman enemy that was hard on our heels. We paused for a moment and took stock. We could hear the pandemonium above but with the fire raging it was very unlikely that our position would be discovered. Furthermore, the booty of the Ark of the Covenant and the menorah, both in symbolism and in weight of gold, would satisfy the greed of Titus, commander of the Roman legions; this would distract them from a closer search of the interior of the sanctuary. We were standing in a secret entrance to King Herod's tunnel that stretched northward to his fortress and southward in the direction of the outer courtyards of the temple complex. The ends of the tunnels disappeared in the gloom as our oil lamps showed no more than twenty or thirty paces in each direction. At our feet were the two bundles we had seen earlier, bound together with leather thongs.*

*We unfurled these bundles and found, as promised, two sets of men's clothing, which we put on. We looked at each other. With our shorn hair and in breeches and tabards we resembled handsome adolescent youths. Also, within the bundles, we discovered goatskins filled with water, which we drank greedily. Finally, in another leather purse, we discovered 100 shekels. Using the sheepskins and the leather thongs we fabricated backpacks to carry our burden of gold and ancient stones of faith and set off south, carefully watching the ground in front of our feet lest we fall down the sinkhole to Hezekiah's tunnel. We found it quickly enough after about a hundred paces. There was a low wall surmounted by wrought-iron winding gear holding an old wooden bucket. A spider's web hung down, attaching itself to the foot of the iron winding gear and the edges of the wall. Its resident eyed us balefully. This gear suggested that Hezekiah's tunnel had been used to supply water to the city in times of siege, which presented a problem. If the tunnel from the Gihon spring was full of water above the height of our heads, then we were trapped. In our favor was the fact that in the months of Sivan, Tammuz, and Av we expect no rain and Israel had in fact been suffering a drought for longer than that. Peering over the edge of the low parapet we again saw iron footrests disappearing into a deeper hole than that from the sanctuary to Herod's tunnel. Using the flames from our oil lamps to frighten the spider from its post, we brushed aside the gossamer threads of its web and descended about twenty cubits down to a dry and sandy floor. This still was no guarantee of escape as we remembered the stories from the book of Kings about how Hezekiah's workmen constructed the tunnel from the two ends, each at an inclination of a narrow angle. How they met in the middle was a miracle of engineering, but the final result was to provide a reservoir of water in the two limbs of a wide-angled V at the point of their junction. We continued walking southward on the sandy slanting floor. After we had walked about five hundred cubits, we encountered water. At first, we noted that the floor of the tunnel was moist enough to show our footprints, then the water covered our ankles, and finally through the gloom we could see the level of the water reaching the roof.*

*We sat down, holding our heads in despair: to have come this far only to be trapped by the handiwork of Hezekiah's engineers! After a few moments of self-pity, I was restored to my normal state of self-reliance. I then remembered my father's favourite aphorism. "After the fall and the expulsion from the Garden of Eden, the Almighty compensated us with the power of reason and enquiry. From this, we were encouraged to continue his acts of creation, with our science defending our faith."*

*How could our meagre knowledge of mathematics and astronomy help us preserve the will of Hashem as inscribed in the third tablet of stone from Mount Sinai? We had only just mastered the teachings of Pythagoras and Archimedes. But at the thought of those names, I experienced my own eureka moment and with my finger drew a diagram in the wet sand. I then explained to Esther how we might use Euclidian mathematics to work out the distance the tunnel was above head height. "Let us assume that both branches of the tunnel are of similar height and declining from the surface at similar angles. Then following the teachings of Archimedes, that water will find its own level irrespective of the shape of its container—its natural height. The problem is easy to solve. Let alpha describe the height of the tunnel, beta the length of water from its edge by our toes to where it reaches the roof of the tunnel in front of us, and finally, let theta be the angle between the surface of the water and the roof of the tunnel. The gamma—the distance we would have to travel underwater to reach the far end— would be solved by Euclid's equation for the isosceles triangles."*

*It took me about ten minutes to make my calculations, writing with my finger on the damp sand at the edge of the underground lake. It was also reassuring to remember our father's parchment that gave us 1,200 cubits from the sinkhole of the spider to the mouth of the tunnel. With relief, the answer came out as 12 cubits— surely not too far to travel on one deep held breath. After explaining all this to Esther I suggested that we practise holding our breath while carrying our loads and walking twelve long strides. "I will test my calculations by walking six strides forward and on my seventh stride judge whether the tunnel has flattened out and begun to turn upwards. I will do this without my burden to ensure that I have breath for my return." At the last minute I remembered that my buoyancy would make me lose my footing, so to compensate I tied the golden candlesticks so that they dropped below my waist.*

*To my delight, after my fifth stride the angle of the tunnel took an un-doubted change of slope and almost immediately turned upwards so that after only ten strides I felt my head break above the surface of the water and after one more step I felt secure enough to take a deep breath. My lungs filled with musty air that stank of rotting vegetable matter, a not unpleasant change from rotting flesh. However, as anticipated, on opening my eyes it was so black that my eyes ached as they tried adjusting to the dark. I turned around and repeated the exercise, emerging triumphantly into the light. Esther fell into my arms with tears of relief blotching her lovely face. Without pausing for words, we set about strapping our burdens so that all our treasures, both worldly and celestial, hung below our waists.*

*This time it took twelve paces and we were desperate for air as we surfaced on the other side of the water trap and the junction of Hezekiah's tunnel. In pitch darkness we staggered on like blind women, feeling our way along the walls until after what seemed a lifetime a glimmer of blessed light appeared as an expanding dot at the limit of our vision. With a bit more bounce in our steps but with increasing exhaustion from our heavy burden, we approached the source of the light at the mouth of the tunnel. It crossed my mind that after all the excitement of our escape had died down and had effectively been quenched by the cold water of the tunnel, the magical power of the word of the Lord as transcribed onto the third tablet of stone no longer had the power to carry us forward but relied on us mere mortals to carry the burden unaided. At last we stumbled through the mouth of the tunnel at the Gihon spring in the Kidron Valley. Blinded by the bright summer sun we fell into the arms of two heavily armed Roman legionnaires. Without hesitation, as if expecting us, they pulled sacks over our head.*

CHAPTER *22*

# RETAKING THE TEMPLE MOUNT

O NCE everyone had finished reading Yehudit's remarkable testament, a deep sigh reverberated around the War Room, and then Naftali Bennet spoke. "Professor Cohen, thanks for this, we will send a couple of our frogmen from the *Shayetet* 13 unit of our navy, to reconnoitre the route from the entrance to Hezekiah's tunnel at Gihon Spring.

Using the guidance provided by this codex we will work on a plan to see if it is credible to launch a surprise attack from within the Dome of the Rock. Once again, my deep thanks but I must now ask you to leave as we finalize our strategy to retake the Temple mount. I know how you must feel to have your wife as a hostage to these evil men, but you will be proud of your son who will have an important role in rescuing the three hostages."

After Professor Daniel Cohen left the room, Prime Minister, took control again.

Turning to the Deputy Chief of staff he issued a list of commands. "Uri, number one get a squad of your frogmen and equip them with audiovisual equipment so that we can follow their journey along the route from the opening of Hezekiah's tunnel and then get one of your technical staff to create a map in three dimensions of the route to the Temple floor translating cubits into meters. As soon as they are ready to go alert me and beam up their journey to this room. If the route runs out along the way, get your Sappers to work out which section of Hezekiah's tunnel is nearest to the walls of the Dome and whether we can blast a hole through to the plateau to take the enemy by surprise. That will be plan B. Then deploy two companies from the crack regiments of Central Command to be in place to storm the walls on the west and south of the Temple mount. They will need siege ladders just like in the good old days of the Titus and Vespasian."

He then turned to the chief of the IAF, "Yosef, fuel up and weaponize a squadron of Apache attack helicopters and call up a company of the parachute reserves from central command to be ready to attack once the 48-hour deadline runs out. The company will be briefed and led by Captain David Cohen who will stay behind for now as I have another task for him. In the meantime, I have a group of experts trying to communicate with our enemy to try and negotiate an extension of their deadline." He nodded to General Uri Ben Shomrim and his friend Yosef Nissan, who saluted and left the room.

He then turned to his attention and addressed his words to the President of the Palestinian authority. "Mr Ben Sadat, your people and my people have been at war since 1948. There has been much blood lost on both sides any many innocents have died in warfare conducted in an urban environment. There is much hatred between us and we each have our own narratives in apportioning blame to the other.

Your predecessor was a weak man who tried in a futile way to please all the people all the time and I know for a fact that he feared assassination at the very thought of negotiation with our side. You are made of sterner stuff and my colleagues in Shin Bet tell me you are well protected from your own people and not a man to be messed with.

You have rose up your ranks as a soldier not as a desk man in a suit, you have proved your metal in leading a branch of the PLO and have served time in our prisons. I'm not asking you to be my friend, but I want to persuade you that we have common purpose and our brothers in arms. The mere fact that you are seated here and sharing our secrets should be proof enough. As a man who has fought battles against us, I'm sure that you have noticed that our plans leave our east flank unprotected. That is why I have invited you here. Shin Bet is well aware that in preparation for the next intifada, should the settlers have had their way in the annexation of the West Bank, you have about 300 fighters armed with assault rifles and rocket-propelled grenades. I'm asking you to mobilize your men and protect our east flank and if needed to break the siege of your holy sanctuaries. It is not only the Dome of the Rock at risk but the third most holy site of Islam, the Al-Asqa Mosque. We want you to share with us the risk and the potential benefits of the battle we're about to enjoin in the next 48 hours."

Marwan Ben Sadat had a spark of intelligence in his dark brown eyes that lit up as he considered the offer. He was a man of small stature but with the charisma that he once shared with Yasser Arafat. His answer was short and to the point, "And if we accept this generous offer Mr. Prime Minister, and if we succeed in winning back that which was ours in the first place, what reward would you offer my people?"

Naftali Bennet replied without a pause, "I had anticipated that question and before coming to this room I had an urgent meeting with President Herzog, the speaker of the Knesset Yariv Levin, and the chairman of the Arab joint list in parliament, Ayman Assad. I am permitted to tell you that we would agree to share Jerusalem as the capital of Israel and the emergent state of Palestine. The idea of annexation of the West Bank will be buried forever and with those promises start negotiations for the Two-State solution.

The other point you need to consider is that if we win the battle, the right-wing extremists in the Knesset will be defanged, although they have not declared in favour of the zealots threatening our holy sites, our electorate will blame them by association, and I can see that the profile of our parliament will turn to face the centre ground."

After another few moments of contemplation, Mr. Ben Sadat stood up and crossed the floor and face to face declared, "It's a deal!" They shook hands and as if by instinct embraced each other in brotherly love. "I will go to alert my men and await your command to deploy them as you suggest." As he was escorted out of the room everyone stood up and clapped their hands. Once they had sat down the Prime Minister turned to the one woman in the room, Shoshana Dayan, the grand-daughter of the legendary one-eyed General Moishe Dayan, the director of the secret service arm, Shin Bet, "Thank you, Shoshana, without that intelligence about his armed guard we would never have achieved that breakthrough. How did you discover all that?"

"Oh, that was easy Naftali, one of his elite fighters is one of our agents. His name is a closely guarded secret but suffice it to know he grew up in the black tents of a Bedouin encampment just south of Beer Sheba and has been a 'sleeper' for 7 years."

"Why am I not surprised?" replied the PM with heavy irony, "Let's take a break for refreshments whilst we wait to learn if it's plan A or plan B.

Jessie, Sophie and Chloe quickly learned that it was futile to kick and scream in their hessian sacks whilst their ankles were tied tightly with a cord that cut into their flesh with every bump along the road in the darkness of the interior of a truck. Chloe was close to panic with a combination of feral fear and the sense of asphyxiation as she tried to breathe through the dense weave of the sack. All three settled down quietly, totally unaware of what was going on. They couldn't have been taken for ransom to be traded of for large sums of money as they weren't that rich and, in any case, why would the IDF be involved in that sort of crime. Independently they settled for the comforting explanation of mistaken identity and how there would be hell to pay when the mistake was discovered. Jessie who knew Jerusalem like the back of her hand, guessed that they were heading east but beyond that had no idea. The end of their journey was a steep climb over what felt like an unstable bridge shortly after which they came to a halt. The tail gate of the truck was dropped, and they were handed down like bundles of grain to hands waiting below. Each of them was carried on the shoulders of big men and gently laid down on a carpeted floor. The cords on their ankles were cut loose and the sacs lifted off their heads. What they then saw was beyond any possible expectation. They appeared to be inside a Church or a Mosque with hexagonal walls, lying on Persian carpets on top of a marble floor. Once their eyes adjusted to the light, they noted that the walls were covered in perfectly executed Arabic writing. Jessie quickly deduced that this was the interior of the sanctuary, the Dome of the Rock. The next thing she deduced was that they were indeed hostages not taken for ransom but as bargaining chips for terrorist.

Three men appeared in front of her eyes as black silhouettes against the bright sunlight shining through the stained glass of the windows of the Mosque. The three men then bent down to lift them up so they could sit with their backs resting against large cushions elaborately decorated in gold braid. She gasped with surprise. They were not the anticipated stereotype Islamic terrorists in beards, baggy trousers, turbans and suicide vests, they look more like the members of the casts of the popular TV series, Shtisel.

In fact, one was the spitting image of the heart throb hero, Akiva.

Then the alpha male of the group spoke out. The three hostages could figure that out simply by the fact that he spoke with a low-pitched voice and the ponderous tone of a man he believes he has leadership qualities.

"Let me tell you who I am. My name is Reb Moishe Ben Levy, and I am the leader of the Shabtai Zvi sect. We have a million followers and at this time we command the Temple Mount. We demand the building of the Third Temple at this site and if our wish is not granted, we will destroy the Dome of the Rock in which we are now holding you hostage. You will be of course the first to die but there will be countless others if our demands are not met as the destruction of the Muslim holy shrines will trigger off a war that can only end by the use of nuclear weapons and the end of the world as we know it.

You can now help us in our task by making a video proving that we have you safe and sound and then plead with your loved ones to do as they are commanded."

Jessie Cohen replied immediately with steel in her words.

"Do you know who I am Mr. Levy?"

"Yes of course, you are the wife of Professor Daniel Cohen of the He-brew University."

"Typical of all you black hated misogynists who expect nothing more of your women than to be breeding machines." Responded Jessie through gritted teeth.

"I am more than a wife I am a person in my own right. I was born Ye-hudit Esther bat Ha'Cohen *hagodal*. My mother was Sara Zenati. My father was Professor Martin Tanner who discovered the Third Tablet of the Holy Covenant. My lineage dates back to the Cohanim of the Second Temple as proven by the records kept in the Zenati synagogue in Peki'in. My mother discovered the scrolls that told the tale of the end of the Second Temple. I am also a Professor at the Hebrew University, but clearly, academic achieve-ments mean nothing to you. So, I, Yehudit Esther bat Ha'Cohen *hagodal*, command you Mr Levy, descendent of a mere servant to the Cohanim, to let us free and go back to your hut in the Shtetl of Meir Sharim." At that Moishe ben Levy went ballistic and screamed at the others to bind Jessie's hands behind her back a seal her mouth with a broad strip of sticky tape.

Once her mouth had been sealed ben Levy's sinister voice changed key as he whispered into Sophie's ear, "I know who you are Mrs Abrahams, you are the wife of the heretic, Professor Robert Abrahams. It would be only right and proper if you were stoned to death rather than waiting for Armageddon."

Sophie was deaf to those words as she and Chloe were still in a state of shock and meekly, like sleepwalkers, did what they were told, and that video recording went viral on all the television news channels in the world.

✻ ✻ ✻

Five hours later, back in the War Room, the reconnoitre of Hezekiah's tunnel had begun. Two frogmen in wet suits but without flippers were at the ready with masks and a cylinder of air on their backs. They were provided with strong torchlights and night vision glasses they were also trailing a long line of fibre optic threads to feed-back audio-visual intelligence. The squad was supported by three technicians monitoring progress in case their plans had to change at the last minute. The monitor in the command centre came alive and the elliptical brick entrance to the tunnel built about 2,700 years earlier was seen in high definition. Soon enough and as expected following the heavy rains in February, the view was continued underwater. As predicted by the Yehudit Codex they soon resurfaced to dry land. Measuring out the distance from the bottom of the sump in the tunnel with one cubit converted to 45 cm, they arrived at the point where they expected to find the bottom of the well from King Herod's tunnel would appear. They soon found what looked like the rusted remains of footrests. Digging around in the debris of bird nests, lichen, fungi and mould, they soon found a vertical cylindrical hole. They leaned a collapsible ladder to the wall of the ancient well and the lead frogman quickly skipped up to the tunnel at the next level. From there it was easy going until they came to the point where they expected to look up and see the hidden entrance to the Holy of Holies. The two naval men, although self-declared atheists, felt the hairs rising on their necks at the thought they were standing just below the resting place of the Ark of the Covenant. There was no obvious opening so, as prepared, they covered the flat surface above their heads with an intense beam of powerful ultrasound normally used by Israel's nuclear submarines in stalking their enemies.

Back in the command center, a cheer went up. The picture projected suggested that the gap between their men and the floor above was only 70 cm thick. That might account for two layers of flagstones and one carpet. Even without finding the swinging flagstone, one blast from a limpet mine would give them entry.

Plan A was ready to be launched.

All the members of the Prime Minister's Command HQ left the room to attend to the details of the attack that was planned for 0400 the next morning. At that precise time, the plateau would be covered by floodlights hidden from view on the flanks and from the helicopters that gathered above the epicentre of the battle to come.

As Captain David Cohen was leaving to join his squadron, the Prime Minister caught his elbow and pulled him back. A complete stranger, grey-haired and bent, was then ushered in and simply introduced as a specialist operative from Mossad.

"Listen carefully Captain Cohen and do everything this man from Mossad tells you. He is my secret weapon. He looks like a tired old man, but his brain and his power of invention in times of war are second to none. He's a bit like Q for quartermaster, in the James Bond movies. We worked closely together when I was head of a commando group during our incursions into Lebanon in the 1990s.

Your mission was to fly above the Temple mount in four Apache attack helicopters. As they blast away with their machine guns, 6 of your men in each chopper were to abseil down into a close contact fight with you in the lead. I am not in the habit of ordering my men into suicide missions. My old quartermaster here has developed a very convincing 'paradummy' a deception device invented by the British during the second world war.

Apart from the pilot, co-pilot and gunner of the Apache, I want you and three others of your command to launch the dummy abseiling soldiers in a way that Q has shown to be convincing. These dummies will be shot to pieces, they will spurt artificial blood and like a scary china doll, they will emit convincing screams. You can now understand why no one else, however well-intentioned, can be part of the subterfuge."

With a big grin on his face, Captain Dave gave a smart salute and followed Q out of the War Room to the quartermaster's store at a level lower than the command centre.

At a time before sunrise and whilst the interior of the Dome of the Rock was in pitch darkness except for the pale light illuminating the niche of the Mihrab pointing towards Mecca, there was a sudden explosion that woke the three hostages from dreaming nightmares to a living nightmare in their immediate proximity. The explosion was followed by billowing smoke lit up by the brilliant light of burning aluminium strips from flash-bang grenades. This was accompanied by an amplified voice shouting, "Bow down, prostrate yourselves this is the voice of the Lord" repeated again and again.

It appeared to come from nowhere or everywhere. Then dark silhouettes of men bending over appeared lit from behind, who seemed to be swarming out of the ground in large numbers of beetles. Jessie, Sophie and Chloe, joined in the screaming that only added to the bedlam, and as commanded laid prostrate on the floor. Their captors, only three in number, were completely disorientated and ran screaming, headlong for the doors.

As the doors flew open, the interior of the sanctuary was flooded with bright light and the sound of gunfire and explosions.

Chloe kept on screaming but the other two women came quickly to their senses and realised they had been saved and were not about to be dragged down to hell like the finale of "The Temptation of Faust."

One of the saviours who had been given the task, having grown up in England, knelt by their side and spoke the most beautiful words they had ever heard even though he had a Geordie accent, "Never yo mind canny lassie no harm will come to yo. Stay still and quiet and yon man with oak leaves on his shoulders will pay yo a visit shortly and explain what the fuck is goin on!"

Captain Cohen Gathered his company together at midnight at IAF base 8 Tel Nof near Rehovot. They had four Apache helicopters on standby, and their crew were busy refuelling the choppers and loading ammunition. There were six parachutists scheduled to be carried by each of the helicopters and it wasn't until the last moment that their leader explained the plan of attack. 5 paras were relieved of their duties from each of the three helicopters leaving one non-commissioned officer to join the flight crew and Captain Cohen in command from the 4th. It was only at that point he was able to explain how they were going to deploy dummy parachutists in order to distract the defenders of the Temple Mount. Those who were relieved of their duties were almost in tears with relief as they had assumed, they were being sent on a suicide mission. They were all fascinated by the dummy parachutists that were going to take their place. In principle, it was an extremely simple ruse. Four strong ropes were attached to ring bolts on the floor of the helicopter. Each of these would carry four fake combatants strung out at different lengths so as to create the illusion of a company of soldiers abseiling down from the open door of the chopper. Each of the dummies carried a tank of fake blood and gunpowder caps in the tunics that would be detonated at intervals to suggest hits from rifle bullets just like a shoot-out in a western movie.

Timing was critical as their attack had to be synchronised as a distraction just before the main attack force burst out of the Dome of the Rock. The flight crew were alerted to hold their fire for fear of blue on blue casualties but instead to play a recording of M230 chain guns. They were also ordered to turn on the floodlights from the undercarriage of the ship the moment they showed themselves rising over the south wall of the Temple mount close to the Al-Asqa Mosque. At 03.30 they got the coded signal that the underground attack squad was in place and ready to go. At 03.50 the four Apaches rose from their base 8 and flying low arrived at their destination at 03.58. They rose slowly above the walls of the citadel as if controlled by strings in the hands of a great puppeteer in the heavens, moved forward until they were just to the north side of the Al Asqa Mosque, turned on their floodlights, let down the dummy combatants and then all hell broke out.

They had no idea of the success of their mission, but one Apache helicopter was lost to an RPG just as they turned south with their mission complete.

Daniel and Robert witnessed the battle from the Al-Buraq Plaza. A Buraq is a mythical white beast with wings on its sides. Some say the beast had the head of a woman and the tail of a peacock. Burāq was originally introduced into the story of Muhammad's night journey from Mecca to Jerusalem and back, thus explaining how the journey between the cities could have been completed in a single night. As the tale of the night journey became connected with that of Muhammad's ascension to heaven from the rock within the Dome. They needed a miracle like this to save their wives and young Chloe.

Once they had learnt of the fate of their wives together with Robert's daughter, they went wild trying to make contact with anyone who might have any idea of what was going on. Obviously, there had been a complete lockdown of IT systems linking the lay public and the arms of the military and the government. Daniel knew that his son would be embroiled in any response and couldn't contact him until the crisis was over. He also knew, with sickening certainty, that Israel never negotiated the release of hostages and inevitably there would be some kind of battle reminiscent of the Entebbe rescue mission in 1976. He kept that knowledge to himself.

They soon got tired of the constant replays of loops of film footage, and the interviews with so-called experts who knew little more than themselves. It was soon obvious that those who were in the know kept shtum and the constant reassurances from the government's spokesmen didn't reassure them a bit. They had therefore decided at midnight to watch the Temple mount from the plaza in the old city with the best view, knowing that they could still watch Sky News on their smartphones and would be alerted if there was any meaningful news. They were not alone in making this decision and found the area cordoned off by the police. Daniel quickly identified the officer in charge and flashed his identity card. The man saluted and let them through for a grandstand view. Robert looked on with surprise as they ducked under the red and yellow tape that defined the out of bounds zone. His companion then modestly explained that he was a reserve *Sgan Aluf* (Lieutenant-Colonel) in the intelligence division of the IDF. They settled down on folding chairs and flasks of coffee to keep them awake and their smartphones in their pockets. The sky was clear and full of stars. If the stars looked brighter in was only because the moon was a mere crescent and all the lights in the Old City in the region of the Western wall and on the Temple mount had been shut down. The only sign of activity was the glimmer of cigarette tips from the occupation militia.

They were just dozing off when at precisely 04.00 the plateau in front of them lit up like the stage set of Götterdämmerung. A fraction of a second later the sound waves hit them.

First, there was a loud explosion near to the north side of the Temple mount, then the chatter of gunfire from the south. Four helicopters were then seen hovering above the centre of the stage and combatants started abseiling from their interiors. At the same time, the doors to the Dome of the rock flew open and three armed men followed by a large squad of militia in black uniforms followed them. Billows of smoke followed these armed men. The abseiling soldiers were shot to pieces and their screams could be from their standpoint. Their binoculars magnified the gory view of blood spouting out of the brave men dropping into a field of heavily armed men. One of the helicopters crashed and three others escaped in a southerly direction. And then more troops appeared out of nowhere from the east of the battlefield and made a run towards the corpses of the parachute brigade screaming curses in Arabic. As suddenly as it started it stopped and the silence was deafening. The reactions from the two men could not have been different.

Robert was inconsolable and sobbing with tears running down his face. Daniel was jubilant and punching the air. Whilst Robert was bending over hands-on face, Daniel's binoculars were focused on the entry to the Dome of the Rock. Exactly as he had expected he witnessed Jessie, Sophie and Chloe being led out by a couple of officers. A team of paramedics ran over and wrapped the three women in foil illuminated by floodlight to look if they were wrapped in silver. A medical officer checked them over and then they were offered hot drinks. It took a lot of effort for Daniel to calm Robert and convince him about the interpretation of the drama he had just witnessed. He was of course aware of plan A with an attack via Hezekiah's tunnel and as the intelligence officer working with the PM during the withdrawal from Lebanon, he had been party to the secret of dummy parachute jumps. They drank the dregs of coffee from their flasks and waited for a call. He assumed it would be from his son if he had survived but he was not sure who had been lost as the Apache went down. They didn't have to wait long. The call came through from the Prime Minister himself with the most beautiful words in the Hebrew language, *"Kol be'seder"*, which literally means all is in order. His plan for an attack through the tunnel worked according to plan. Their attack on the terrorists was not just from the rear but from the underground as well. As guessed the abseiling soldiers were all dummies that worked to distract the enemy from the real direction of the assault. They had only lost two men who were on the crew of the Apache that went down, and his courageous son was safe and well and being debriefed at this very moment

A few hours later yet still only 09.00 the same morning, the two families were reunited at number A4 in Yamin Moishe. The womenfolk were accompanied by two paramedics and a counsellor trained to care for hostages and other innocents caught in the collateral damage of warfare. The two men had already found comfort in two fingers of fine malt whiskey. Chloe was in tears and Jessie & Sophie were pallid and still shaking with fear.

An hour later the dishevelled and exhausted figure of David Cohen crashed through the doors and into the arms of his parents. Not long after that, there was another knock on the door that when opened revealed two heavy-set men in suits who quickly scanned the room before allowing the Prime Minister into the sitting room. Although to be honest, they were long past caring, they all stood up in respect except for Chloe whose legs were like jelly and in any case had no idea of the identity of the new stranger.

In haste and with little formality, the Prime Minister spoke. "I've come straight from my war room once we had confirmed the outcome of this impossible mission and the first two people I need to thank are you, Daniel and David Cohen. Thanks to the pair of you we have won back control of the Temple mount, the three hostages have been set free unharmed, and the terrorists led by Moishe ben Levy have all been killed or have given themselves up. Ben Levy attempted to escape over the eastern wall but is now in the hands of our colleagues from the PLO, who have been asked to treat him kindly. We have lost one Helicopter and its crew, three of our infantrymen but still not sure of the losses amongst the fighters of the PLO. None of this would be possible without learning about the tunnel that led our forces to the interior of the Dome of the Rock." Then turning to Captain David Cohen, he added, "Your courage in leading the deceptive attack by air that had the terrorist looking the wrong way will win you the highest military award the state can offer"

CHAPTER 23

# THE AFTERMATH

O NCE the dust had settled on the Temple mount both literally and figuratively, matters on the domestic and geopolitical scene moved rapidly.

Shin Bet rounded up all the members of the Shabtai Zvi sect. Those who were visitors from the UK & USA were put on the next flight home.

The survivors amongst their fighters were tried in the Supreme Court and given long sentences if they were found guilty of being traitors. Some of the naïve kids under the age of 19, were sent off for training as infantrymen in the IDF. The UK and the USA proscribed the group as a terrorist organization. Both chief Rabbis resigned, and their successors lifted the *herem* curse from Professor Abrahams who was also offered citizenship should he ever decide to make *Aliyah*. Cohen, father and son, were both awarded the medal of valour. The three hostages were each awarded the President's medal in a very moving ceremony at Yad Vashem. Chloe was offered a place at the Hebrew University in Jerusalem to study archaeology. She was quick to accept that offer as it allowed her the chance for the development of a relationship with Captain Dave even though he was nearly 8 years older than her.

Perhaps of greater Importance than all these happy events were the shifts in the tectonic plates of middle eastern politics. This was kicked off when the Prime Minister called a snap general election. The extreme right-wing parties were wiped out as predicted, Likud did very badly and at last, a strong centre-left democracy emerged that was supported by the joint Arab list.

The new plan for a two-state solution was sketched out by the new Israeli Cabinet and the leaders of the reformed Palestinian authority (PA) and a President, Mr Ben Sadat who had his back covered. No foreign power was called in to convene or chair the deliberations. As Gaza was still ruled by an intransigent oligarchy from Hamas, they were left out of the equation. The deal involved was simplicity itself. To start with Jerusalem was to be the capital to be shared by both states with the Palestinian house of representatives moved from Nablus to East Jerusalem. Control of the Temple mount would continue under the aegis of the Waqf and given International status like the Vatican in Rome.

Minor exchanges of disputed land at the old green line were made as *quid pro quo* but the masterstroke was to declare the so-called settlements as *villages* whereby chance, a majority were of the Jewish faith. They would be fully integrated into the new State of Palestine but there was no reason why those of the Muslim faith couldn't live in these villages as well. This was no different to the many Arab villages scattered around Israel. If you drive in the hills of Galilee, you will more than often see the minarets of Mosques rather than the domes of synagogues. Those Jews who didn't like it could travel west and live in Israel.

Although not allowed a standing army the PA could arm their police force and border control officers. Anyone bearing a passport from either side of the border would be allowed free passage without harassment. This was risk-free because the old PLO was now the new border control gendarmes, and the two countries were to share intelligence linked to operatives from Hamas and Hezbollah.

The two states would be trading parties without tariffs and offered neighbouring states to join this trading union. What with the start-ups in Israel's Silicon Valley and the discovery of oil offshore (Or as Winston Churchill once said "a prize from fairyland far beyond our brightest hopes") prosperity would be guaranteed for this new bloc once Peace broke out!

What about the noisy neighbours though? Jordan to the East and Egypt to the South were already on good terms with Israel and the nascent new State of Palestine. The Abrahamic accord with the Gulf States was already in place.

It was hoped that with the growing prosperity on the West Bank, the poor suffering common folk in Gaza might rise against their de facto rulers, Hamas. Time would tell but intelligence gathered by Mossad and the PA secret service suggested that time needed a little tweak from their agents in the strip.

In the north, Lebanon was an ungovernable failed state but at least Hezbollah was being blamed for their problems. It was likely that under UN law, the French army would be invited by the interim government to control all the fighting factions and drag the country to the ballot box whilst locking up the most corrupt of the old governing clique.

To the northeast was an open ulcer that would never heal. What was once the centre of the Assyrian Empire was now a basket case beyond repair. It was about time the Sykes/Picot line in the sand was redrawn and the UN blue helmets were sent in to take control. Opinion in Israel put money on the bet that the Messiah would come first.

Needless to say, in the fullness of time, the Prime Minister of Israel and the President of Palestine would be invited to Stockholm to share the Nobel Peace Prize.

# The Cairo Museum

Passover began on the evening of Saturday the 27th of March. There was no question of us flying back home after the traumas we had experienced, so Sophie, Chloe and myself stayed on for another week to live through all 7 days of the festival. We would eat matzah; the bread of affliction and I would deny myself malt whiskeys that included forbidden grain. In its place I would drink kosher vodka to settle my nerves.

The State of Israel would cover our expenses and we continued staying in our apartment overlooking the Kidron valley and the walls of the Old City. In addition, my wife and daughter were required to help the police by making statements that described their experiences in the hands of the terrorists, to help them plan a case for the prosecution.

The last day of the festival was April 3rd and as chance would have it, the Nefertiti exhibition was being transported to Cairo that very week, having completed its three-month sojourn at the British Museum. The opening of the exhibition had been planned to coincide with the formal opening of the new Egyptian State Museum of Archaeology (ESMA), which would replace the tired old home of the Tutankhamen treasure trove and all the other artefacts of the great Kings and Queens of this ancient culture stretching back to the 5th C BCE.

All the great and the good in this field of study would be there including the President of Egypt and The Prince of Wales. There was to be a contingent from Israel that included Professors Daniel and Jessie Cohen.

I had been offered accommodation in Professor in Professor Sharif's compound at Saqqara, who insisted that my wife and daughter accompanied me. I thought this would make a wonderful distraction for them and a true holiday away from the scene of the terrible experience. A quick phone call to the headmistress of Chloe's school settled the matter as this wise woman was quick to point out that her student would learn more in the field than behind her desk at the JFS.

For the eve of Passover, we were invited again to the home of Daniel and Jessie next door to Montefiore's old windmill. In Israel, they only celebrate one *Seder* night, unlike the diaspora where we repeat it. *Seder* night, since my childhood, has been my favourite festival. It is a family affair than can sometimes stretch to midnight by which time the youngest children are asleep on the floor. The event is stratified into pre-dinner prayers, dinner and post-dinner prayers. For most of us is the main attraction, was dinner, with up to 7 different dishes of traditional recipes. In north London, we enjoy a heavy Ashkenazi cuisine whilst in Israel, we were treated to a more exotic, middle eastern, Sephardi cuisine. The rituals start when the youngest male stands on a chair to ask the four questions that start, "Why is this night different to all other nights?"

The answer to that simple question usually takes about four hours with a break for dinner. Essentially it is the retelling of the Biblical narrative of the Exodus from Egypt.

I am well aware of my cognitive dissonance in enjoying the Bible story whilst denying its authenticity. At intervals, through the evening we are commanded to drink four goblets of wine. In London, this is a hardship as the kosher wine is almost undrinkable whilst in Israel, the vineyards on the Golan Heights, produce some of the finest wines in the world. At one point in the rituals, we recite the 10 plagues, spilling one drop of wine for each plague in memory of the suffering of the innocent ancient Egyptians at that time. Even though I have a rational explanation for each "plague", I find this gesture deeply moving. The end of the service involves singing traditional songs that have appeared as accretions over the last 1,500 years, to the service as written in our little illustrated handbooks known as the *Hagadah*. Shortly before the end of the service, we all sing to a beautiful melody, *L'shana haba b'Yerushalyim, which* simply translated means, "May next year be in Jerusalem". To sing this in the diaspora has some meaning but why sing it in Jerusalem? The best explanation is in the translation of Jerusalem from Biblical Hebrew into modern English. *Yr ha'shalom* means the City of Peace. After what we had been through, I had never sung that prayer with such unrestrained passion whilst looking at my wife and daughter and breaking down with uncontrollable tears.

ESMA has to be the most beautiful modern museum in the world in spite of being over-budget and years overdue. Yet to formally open the museum with a new exhibition celebrating the most iconic figure in the history of Egyptology, could not have been more appropriate. The Spring weather was perfect and our contingent responsible for the discoveries at Saqqara, were given seats in the second tier of the temporary terraced seating forming a semicircle in the plaza facing the new building. My wife and daughter were by my side. For an hour we enjoyed the marching bands and the display of traditional dancing in traditional costumes. Next the dignitaries came out to speak, each one full of self-importance and running over time. HRH, Charles Prince of Wales, did a splendid job in describing how Egyptology was born thanks to the adventurists, many of whom were women, during the late Victorian era. He explained that the prominence given to the British contingent was not so much because of the Brits in our time, but because the very subject of Egyptology was started by British adventurers at the time Egypt was a protectorate not to mention the fact that Lord Carnarvon Howard Carter unearthed the mummy and treasures of King Tut.

After the tape was cut by President Abdel Fattah Al-Sisi, the VIPs including my little family traipsed in and were conducted around the exhibition. They had made a fantastic job on the display using natural light from above for most exhibits and subtle artificial coloured lighting from below for the small artefacts and the precious stones, scarabs and amulets. However, the star of the show I had never seen before.

Professor Caroline Wilkinson, of Liverpool John Moores University, who had achieved fame in reconstructing the head from the remains of King Richard III, had carried out the same procedure on the skull of Nefertiti, unearthed at Saqqara. This turned out to be an almost perfect replica of the regal head of Nefertiti made by Tuthmose, the artist to the Royal Household nearly 3,500 years ago.

The symposium that followed was in a splendid new lecture theatre with all mod cons.

Every seat was a red leather armchair fronted by a cedar wood desktop with its own microphone and a small screen that showed the slides together with subtitles in English or Arabic as required. The programme went ahead almost exactly as in London, with a few surprising additions.

As a codicil to my paper, I was able to confirm that the RNA signature of the virus that caused the plague that decimated the citizens of Amarna, was identical to the one that caused havoc all over the world and was yet still endemic in parts of South America, Texas, Mumbai, and some sub-Saharan nations. If anything, this was the curse of the Pharaohs. How this virus survived inert or hosted by non-human species, only to re-emerge in China in 2019, was a mystery. I loved solving mysteries and this challenge might help us to understand and control the virus for good.

Jessie Cohen was a new speaker and as the world authority on the BRCAI mutation, she had been given the task of trying to explain how this mutation was shared between Nefertiti and herself. Very few people knew that she had inherited the mutation from her mother, a member of the Zenati family who had carried the curse for at least 2,000 years.

A mutation like this, which killed 80% of women before menopause, could have the opposite of a survival advantage. But her seminal work on the gene controlling fractal geometry demonstrated co-expression that was expressed in the perfect vasculature of the placenta. She also liked to mythologise the idea that her line emerged from the relationship between Nefertiti and her court artist.

The last speaker was Lucy Carpenter, and I would like to show the transcript of her closing speech.

"Mr President, your Royal Highness, Lords, Ladies and friends,

I'm honoured by this invitation to close this assembly as my contribution to the discoveries and their interpretation, of the three mummies discovered in Professor Abdul Sharif's back yard, were relatively modest. We gather here just a few days from the unspeakable crime of religious fanatics who invaded one of the holiest sites belonging to all the Abrahamic religions in the world today. These evil men can be described as fundamentalists who believe in the strict, literal interpretation of the scriptures. Left to their own devices they might have destroyed two of the holiest Muslim sanctuaries in the world. They also took hostages, who, thank God, are sitting in this auditorium today. The outcome of the retaking of the Temple mount, had it failed, might have led to a World War that could be described as Armageddon. The success of the raid to retake the mount can mostly be credited to an archaeologist, Professor Daniel Cohen, who is also sitting amongst us." At this point heads were turning around, this way and the other, searching for the hero and heroines who wisely kept still and expressionless except for the smile of a Mona Lisa smile on Chloe's.

"Archaeology teaches us to understand and learn from the past. The Children of Israel had learnt that a safe supply of water would help them sit out a siege, as important as strong walls. The wisdom of King Hezekiah served us well last week.

Returning to today's event, apart from that discovery of Nefertiti's mummy, that might overshadow the greater importance of our other findings, let me remind you that our discoveries have also overturned the literal interpretation of the Exodus narrative. Does this matter?

The pursuit of an objective truth is the purpose of the scientific method that I respect.

Some of you might have noticed that I used the words, 'thanks to God', that in spite of what you think, was not a cliché. I am not an atheist and I do see 'the hand of God' in certain circumstances. The question 'Do you believe in God?' is a meaningless meme because all who confess to faith have different concepts of the Almighty. It would take too long to describe my own beliefs, but I can illustrate them in this way.

Yes, our science has revisited the story of the Exodus of the Children of Israel. Moses was an Egyptian Prince, who lead a small group of monotheists out of Egypt. His followers were not slaves who built the pyramids, as we confirmed these monuments were built by professional artisans who live in nearby villages. We think that the 40 years in the wilderness is a metaphor to describe the time it took Moses and his fellow priests to get rid of paganism and restore a belief in one God to the pre-existing tribes.

Do these factoids change the eternal and all-encompassing lessons we can learn from the Bible? No is the answer, the Biblical narrative and the Scientific narrative run side by side and are mutually supportive as Chief Rabbi Jonathan Sacks wrote in his book, The Great Partnership, 'Science takes things apart to see how they work. Religion puts things together to see what they mean'. Let me tell you what the Biblical narrative of the Exodus means to me. My grandparents were the children of slaves and as a child sitting on their knees, I learnt what slavery really meant. My grandparents taught me the Bible and taught me how the story of the liberation of the slaves in the time of the Pharaohs gave them hope. My parents suffered badly at the hands of racists when they came to England in the 1950s and were treated like slaves. The Bible story gave them spiritual support. To this day Gospel singers reiterate the spirituals that gave hope to their fore-fathers. I sing in one of those choirs back home on Sundays in my Church and I'm going to sing the first verse and you are all welcome to join in the chorus."

Then in a deep honey-toned contralto voice, she started singing.

*When Israel was in Egypt land*
*Let my people go*
*Oppressed so hard they could not stand*
*Let My people go*

*So Moses went to Egypt land*
*Let My people go*
*He made old Pharaoh understand*
*Let My people go*

*Thus spoke the Lord, bold Moses said*
*Let My people go*
*If not I'll smite your firstborn dead*
*Let My people go*

*Go down Moses way down in Egypt Land*
*Tell old Pharaoh to let My people go.*

## THE END

# Acknowledgements

T HIS book did not leap readymade from my head, it came as a result of reading four books and the catalogue of the exhibition of the underwater archaeology at the British Museum, as described in the first chapter that first inspired me to write this story.

There is no rank order in mentioning the other four books as they were all equally readable and full of amazing facts.

So, in the order in which I read them they are.

"Archaeology of Race" 2013, by Debbie Challis

"The search for Nefertiti" 2004 by Joann Fletcher

"Writings from Ancient Egypt" 2016 compiled and translated by Toby Wilkinson

"The Exodus" 2014 by Richard Elliott

In addition, I must offer personal thanks to David Gerrard to advised me about SCUBA diving and providing me with an avatar thinly disguised as David Goddard.

Finally, my deepest thanks to my good friend, Rabbi Doctor Geoffrey Cohen, who schooled me in the relevant sections of the Talmud and Jewish law and debated with me on the non-binary links between Science and Faith. His avatar is also thinly disguised.

Printed in Great Britain
by Amazon

31957542R00096